SEVEN SLEEPERS **THE LOST CHRONICLES** 1

The Spell of the Crystal Chair

GILBERT MORRIS

MOODY PRESS
CHICAGO

Library of Congress Cataloging-in-Publication Data

Morris, Gilbert.
    The spell of the crystal chair / by Gilbert Morris.
        p. cm. -- (The lost chronicles ; #1)
    Summary: The Seven Sleepers are sent to foil the Dark Lord in
Whiteland where they must destroy a special chair deep inside the
wizard's palace.
    ISBN 0-8024-3667-6 (pbk.)
    [1. Fantasy. 2. Christian life--Fiction.] I. Title.

PZ7.M8279 Sp 2000
[Fic]--dc21

                                                            99-058291

                    1 3 5 7 9 10 8 6 4 2

            Printed in the United States of America

Contents

Prologue
The Lost Chronicles

A laughing girl skimmed as lightly as a deer between the towering trees. She had bright blonde hair and flashing blue eyes and wore a white garment that shimmered when the sun struck it. She was all motion and grace as she evaded the grasp of her companion.

"You're too fast for me, Reena!" The boy smiled at her as they rested beneath an enormous oak. "But it was a good race."

"I've never been in this section of the woods before, Darin." Her gaze moved over the landscape, then she exclaimed, "Oh, look—there's a cave."

"I believe it is—a small one."

"Let's go over and take a look."

They jogged toward the cliff that rose in front of them, a sheer leap of stone into the blue sky. The cave entrance was narrow, but Reena said, "I want to see what's inside! I can squeeze through. You wait here."

For a few moments Darin waited impatiently, and then Reena came wriggling back through the opening. She held a metal box in her hands.

"What's *that?*"

"I don't know. Maybe some treasure from the Old Days!" The box was thickly crusted with reddish mold. "I can tell it's very old," she said. "And it's heavy, for such a small box!"

"Well, let's see what's in it."

Reena placed the box on the ground. There was no lock, and when she pulled sharply at the top, it

5

opened at once. "Why—it's old books!" She reached into the ancient box and held up a volume bound in red leather.

"What in the world are they?"

Reena squinted at the cover. "It says *The Chronicles of the Seven Sleepers—The Spell of the Crystal Chair.*"

"Looks like there's a whole set," Darin exclaimed. But then a puzzled look crossed his face. "I thought we'd heard all the stories of the Seven Sleepers—but I don't remember that one."

"I don't, either." As Reena carefully leafed through the book, a single sheet of paper came free in her hand. "What is this?" She unfolded it and began to read aloud:

I, Gandor, son of Balin, have collected these tales of the Seven Sleepers. Thinking it not good that the noble deeds done by these heroic young people should be forever lost to the world, I have written these adventures as the Sleepers told them to me.

Now the last battle is upon us. Not knowing if I shall live or die, I am placing these chronicles in a metal box. If I survive the last battle against the Dark Lord and his evil forces, I will return and share these with the world. If I do not survive, and they are forever lost, they would be properly called "The Lost Chronicles of the Seven Sleepers."

Now, the trumpets of war are blowing. I go to meet my fate, and we will see if the forces of Goél prevail. If Goél is not the victor—I care not to live.

Thoughtfully, Reena turned back to the opening page of *The Spell of the Crystal Chair.* She read the first few lines silently, then looked at her companion with joy. "Now we will hear of adventures of the Seven Sleepers that have never been sung!"

"And all shall know of the courage of those young people who served Goél when the powers of darkness closed in on Nuworld."

Darin and Reena sat again beneath the oak, and she began to read aloud: "Abbey Roberts knelt beside a small creek washing her hair . . ."

1

A Discontented Crew

A bbey Roberts knelt beside a small creek washing her hair. She was a most attractive girl, thirteen years old. At the moment her long blonde hair was filled with white suds, and for the most part she kept her eyes closed to keep the soap out. From time to time she would open them, though, and glance over at Sarah Collingwood, who sat on the bank, reading a book.

Sarah was only one year older. Her hair was as black as Abbey's was blonde, and her eyes, which were more than half closed with sleepiness just now, were large, brown, and wide-spaced.

The two girls had come away from the rest of the Sleepers to spend some time alone.

There were times when Sarah and Abbey did not get along. They were very different. Abbey spent a great deal of time making herself more attractive, a habit that irritated Sarah considerably.

"You're always primping, Abbey. Don't you ever get tired of trying to make yourself look better?" Sarah had said this more than once, and that irritated Abbey considerably. She always responded, "It's a girl's responsibility to look as good as she can, Sarah. It wouldn't hurt you to take a little bit more care of your hair and to spend a little more time with makeup."

As Abbey got on her hands and knees to let her hair fall forward into the water, she thought, *If we were back in Oldworld, Sarah and I would never be friends at all. We're just too different.*

She splashed the cold water over her hair, keeping her eyes tightly shut, and for a moment her mind went back to the time before the world as all the Sleepers had known it was destroyed by atomic war.

That time was like a dream now. She knew she would probably never see again such things as Popsicles, which she loved, or all the other little things that had filled her world. As she rinsed out the last of the soap, she thought with discontent, *It doesn't do much good to pay attention to your looks here in Nuworld. Nobody's going to see you except maybe some sort of weird mutants like Mat and Tam.*

She squeezed her hair to get the water out, then picked up a towel. It was not really a towel. It was simply a large piece of cloth. As she tried to dry her hair, she wished for a thick, fluffy white towel such as she had used every day before Oldworld disappeared. The cloth seemed a sort of sad symbol of all that she had lost.

Abbey and the other Six Sleepers had been placed in protective capsules before the bombs went off. The seven young people had "slept" for many years. She was not quite sure how many.

When they emerged, the world was different. Geography had gone crazy. Even the continents had changed, for the oceans had washed away many old lands and new ones had been formed. Strange mutant forms had arisen—giants, dragons, dinosaurs . . . Abbey suddenly thought, *No one ever knows what sort of monster he'll meet in Nuworld.*

She longed for the old days. The lives of the Seven Sleepers had been filled with little but hard adventure since they had been awakened. They had become the servants of a strange man called Goél, whom Abbey could never quite figure out. He would appear from time to time, give them orders, and in obedience they would throw themselves into an adventure. Often their lives were at risk, yet Goél seemed as much interested in making them into something different—*better*, he said—as in anything else.

"I guess Goél will be coming along soon to send us on another quest against the Dark Lord, Sarah." She glanced in Sarah's direction.

But Sarah apparently had not heard. The book she had been reading lay in her lap, and her arms had fallen to her side. Abbey knew their last adventure had taken every bit of Sarah's strength. Perhaps the warm sun overhead had been too much for her. She began to slump down.

Abbey's eyes flew wide. "Sarah! Wake up! You're falling in!"

And Sarah Collingwood *was* tilting over. The bank was steep where she sat, and she simply flipped over headfirst in a rather boneless fashion and hit the cold water. The stream closed over her head, and her arms beat at the water as she attempted to come up.

Then Abbey remembered that Sarah was wearing heavy hiking boots. They would fill with water at once and drag her down. *Oh, no!* She thought. *We've been through all sorts of dangers, and now Sarah's going to drown by falling into a creek!*

Upstream from the two girls, Josh Adams sat with a small sapling in his hand. At the end he had tied a stout cord, and a bit of light wood served as a cork. He and the other male members of the Seven Sleepers had decided to come to the creek to fish. They were tired of their monotonous diet.

"I wish I was back home in Arkansas," Bob Lee Jackson said. "I bet I could show you how to catch fish then." Bob Lee was called just Reb by the other Sleepers. He was fourteen, tall and lanky. His light blue eyes were half shaded by the cowboy-style straw hat he wore, and strands of tow-colored hair straggled out from beneath it. "I've been fishing there when the fish bit so good that you had to hide behind a tree to bait your hook."

Josh grinned. "Don't you ever get tired of telling those lies?" He was almost as tall as Reb but was rather skinny, being on the brink of young manhood but still not fully coordinated. Although he had been chosen to be the leader of the Sleepers, Josh was shy and unsure of himself and could not believe he was the leader of anything.

Dave Cooper laughed aloud. At fifteen, he was the oldest of the Sleepers. He was a handsome boy with brown hair and gray eyes and was very athletic. "Back home where I lived, we'd catch fish that weighed twenty or thirty pounds."

"Were they catfish, or is that another one of your educated lies?" Reb sounded suspicious.

"No, we lived right on the Gulf. We'd go out on charter boats. We caught many an amberjack that weighed twenty pounds. Wish I had one now."

The other two members of the group sat side by side, quietly fishing. Jake Garfield, a Jewish boy, was the group's mechanical genius. He could make anything work. Now he nudged the Sleeper beside him, saying, "Hey, Wash, let's get away from here. They're starting to swap those lying fish tales. I don't want to hear it."

Wash—Gregory Randolf Washington Jones—was twelve, the youngest Sleeper. He had ebony black skin and a beautiful white smile. He giggled and lifted his fish hook to examine it. "I wonder which one of them's going to tell the biggest lie about fish."

"I don't think—" Josh Adams began.

And then someone screamed.

Josh threw down his pole and leaped to his feet. "That's Abbey!" he cried and took off at a dead run.

"It sounds bad," Dave said at the same moment, and all of the boys dropped their poles and raced off after Josh.

Josh ignored the brambles that clutched at him. A branch scratched him across one eye, half blinding him. But Abbey's screams were serious, and he sped on. He had toughened up since coming to Nuworld and was not even breathing hard when he burst into the clearing where she stood, pointing down at the water.

"She fell in, Josh! She's drowning!"

Taking in the situation at one swift glance, Josh kicked off his shoes and made a shallow dive into the creek. It was something he would not have done otherwise, for he knew that diving into unknown waters could get a fellow hurt quick. But he saw Sarah struggling and knew there was no time to lose.

The mountain creek closed over him, its coldness taking his breath. He was thankful that swimming had always been his best sport. He came to the surface, his arms pumping and his feet kicking frantically. Just ahead, Sarah's hands broke the surface, and he drove himself toward her. When he reached where she struggled, sinking again, he grabbed a handful of her hair and pulled her head above water.

But Sarah began to clutch at him, threatening to drag them both under.

"Don't grab at me, Sarah! Just let yourself go! Relax, I've got you!"

As is true with most drowning people, Sarah Collingwood was beyond reason. Frantically she kept clutching at Josh.

But he continued carrying her entire weight by her heavy hair. As she sputtered and struggled, he swam strongly, towing her toward shore.

And then he felt his feet touch bottom. "It's OK," he gasped. "You're OK now, Sarah."

But now her heavy hiking boots sank into the mud. Josh put both arms around her and pulled her free, then staggered toward the bank.

"Give me a hand, you guys! She keeps getting stuck in the mud."

Dave jumped in and took hold of Josh's waist, and Jake did the same for Dave. The others formed a human chain, and a tug-of-war with the creek bottom began.

Sarah's feet came out of the squishy mud, but her boots remained there. She was dragged unceremoniously to shore, and as soon as she was there she did a very ungrateful and surprising thing.

Turning around, she slapped at Josh. "Get your hands off me!" she cried.

He stared at her, then looked wildly around at the group. "Get my hands off of you? You would have drowned if I hadn't put my hands on you!"

"No, I wouldn't have! I can swim as good as you can!"

"You didn't look like it," Wash protested. "You looked like a goner to me, Sarah. I think Josh saved your life."

"He's always showing off," she said, next to tears. As a rule, Sarah was very sweet and reasonable, and Josh was sure she liked him. But she lashed out at him verbally now. "I didn't need your help! I was just about ready to kick off my boots and start swimming."

Reb shoved the straw Stetson back on his forehead and grinned broadly. "You sure gave a good imitation of a girl drowning," he said. "You ought to go on the stage and be an actress if you can act that good."

"You hush up, Reb!" Sarah said furiously.

Dave too could not help teasing her a little. "You look like a drowned rat," he said. "What did you do, just jump in to make yourself look funny?"

But then Wash interrupted. "Hey, you guys! Let up a little. That was a pretty bad scene." He went over to Sarah. "That wasn't too funny, was it? That stream's swift. I nearly drowned in it myself the other day. It's worse than the Old Man."

"What old man?" Abbey asked.

"Oh, that's what we used to call the Mississippi River back in Oldworld. I used to just about drown in it every summer."

Sarah, Josh thought, must have felt absolutely stupid. She was looking down at her dripping clothes and her ugly, now black socks, which were covered with mud. Her hair streamed down in her face. She repeated, "I didn't need your help, Josh. I would have gotten out all by myself."

She turned then and ran away as quickly as she could. The stones must have hurt her bare feet, but she paid no attention.

Josh watched as she disappeared. He had known Sarah Collingwood back in Oldworld when she had lived with his family. He had thought then that she was the prettiest girl alive and was in awe of her.

Now as he stood there soaking wet, looking after her, he shook his head. "Girls are sure funny."

Reb took off his hat and ran his hand through his sandy hair. "They sure are. I had this kooky cousin called Mary Belle Smite. She was bigger and stronger than any boy, and she liked to wrestle with the mule we had on our place. She was almost tough enough to throw him down. Most of us figured any girl that could throw a mule down would be too hard on a feller, so she didn't have many boyfriends. She was a funny one."

"Sarah was just scared and embarrassed," Wash said. "Abbey, why don't you go see if she's all right?"

"All right. I will." She looked at Josh with admiration. "You sure can swim, Josh."

Josh basked for a moment in the warmth of her compliment, but as Abbey left them, he shook his head again. "Sarah sure was mad."

Wash was always the peacemaker. He struck Josh lightly on the arm. "Don't worry about Sarah," he said. "Like I said, she was embarrassed. She'll be all right."

"I hope so," Reb grunted. "I'd hate to think she was gonna be that mean and nasty all the time."

Supper that night was a somewhat tense affair. For one thing, Sarah had not gotten into a mood that was much better. She realized that she had done a very stupid thing. Abbey had told her it could happen to anyone, and most of the others had been sympathetic, but she could not see it that way.

She had done the best she could with her hair, but there were no hair dryers in Nuworld, and her hair was long, coming halfway down her back. She'd dried it by simply sitting out in the sun. For supper, she tied it into a long braid. She ate little and said almost nothing.

Then, Reb and Dave got into an argument. Dave had acted as the cook that night, and when Reb tasted the meat, he said, "Dave, you're the worst cook I ever saw. Why, this meat's raw!"

Dave, who did not like to cook anyway and was, in fact, not very good at it, said, "If you don't like it, don't eat it!"

Reb was quick to take offense. "I've seen cows hurt worse than this and still get well," he said. "It ain't fit to eat."

"Will you two calm down?" Wash put in quickly. "Dave did the best he could, Reb."

Josh said little. His eyes kept going to Sarah, as though he was expecting her to apologize or to at least say some kind of thank you. But she sat with her head down, saying nothing.

Finally Josh sat down beside her. "Are you still mad at me?"

Sarah looked up and felt tears coming to her eyes. "I'm—I'm not mad at you, Josh. I just felt so stupid. Imagine, just falling in the river like that! I'm the dumbest girl that ever lived!"

"It could happen to anybody," he said.

She blinked her tears away then and managed a smile. "You're the sweetest boy, Josh."

He lowered his head and said, "Aw, shucks! It wasn't anything!"

"It was, too. I really would have drowned if I couldn't have gotten those old boots off. I guess you saved my life."

"Well, what would I do without you, Sarah?"

17

At that moment, a voice outside caught everybody's attention. Instantly, the Sleepers jumped to their feet. Nuworld was a dangerous place, and they all grabbed weapons—swords, knives, anything. Josh seized a staff with which he had become quite handy. "Who's out there?" he called.

"Why don't you open the door and find out?"

The voice was rough and sounded vaguely familiar. "I know that voice," Josh said. "I just can't place it." He opened the door and gaped in amazement. "Mat," he said, "it's you!"

"And me. Tam. Can we come in? We're starved to death."

Grinning, Josh stepped back. The two strange looking individuals who entered were identical twins. They were not more than three feet tall and were fat as sausages. Their bellies gave promise of exploding any minute were it not for their broad, black leather belts with shiny brass buckles. Both had round red cheeks with small black eyes peering out from under impossibly bushy eyebrows. Both also had bushy beards that covered their chests.

"Well, I don't see much improvement around here," Mat said, scowling. But Tam was going about greeting everyone with a happy smile.

Mat and Tam were Gemini twins, a strange mutant form that had occurred in Nuworld. The Gemini mothers gave birth to twins every time, and the strange thing was that these twins were usually as different inside as they were alike outside. Mat, for instance, was grumpy, always complaining, always seeing the dark side of things, while Tam was the cheerful optimist who saw good in everything.

Mat and Tam were scarcely inside when Tam said,

"Oh, we forgot someone!" He went back to the door and said, "Come on in."

The room suddenly seemed to be filled, for an enormous man stooped and came through the door.

"Volka!" Sarah cried. She ran to him and reached up her arms for a hug. She could not reach the neck of the giant, who stood well over eight feet tall. "Ho," he said, his eyes twinkling, "my Sleeper friends." Volka's voice was as big as his body.

"Here, sit before you knock the ceiling down," Josh said. He waited until Volka was seated on the floor and Tam and Mat were sitting at the table. "Now let's give these fellas something to eat."

The three visitors ate like starving sharks.

After they were finished, Mat said, "Well, it's happened again." His eyes were gloomy, and he hunched his shoulders in despair. "I know it will turn out to be no good."

"Sure it'll be good," Tam said. "I'm glad to be here."

"Me too," Volka boomed. He had cleaned up all the food and sat looking hopefully for more.

"What are you fellows doing here?" Abbey asked. "We didn't expect you to come."

"It's that Goél again," Mat said, a woeful look on his face. "He told us to come here." Then he glared around angrily. "We've got to take care of you babies again!"

"Goél told you to come here?" Josh said, suddenly alert.

"Yes. Worse luck," Mat complained. "To be babysitters."

"What did he tell you to do?" Dave asked, puzzled. All of the Sleepers knew that any message from Goél must be obeyed instantly.

"Didn't say," Mat said. "Just gave us a map and said

to be here. Well, here we are. Now we'll just have to wait until he shows up."

"It'll be fun," Tam said happily. He hit his twin in the side with his elbow. "Cheer up! Things could be worse."

Mat glared at him. "They probably will be."

2
The Word of Goél

None of the Sleepers slept particularly well the night after the Gemini twins and Volka arrived. Josh, as their leader, was more restless, perhaps, than the others. He lay awake for a long time listening to the breathing of his friends grow steady and slow as they finally dropped off into sleep.

What's Goél going to send us into this time? he wondered.

Locking his hands behind his head, Josh stared up at the thatch roof of the hut that had been their home for several weeks. He thought of the dangers that he had encountered simply finding the other six Sleepers. Thoughts of Emas, the chief interrogator for the Dark Lord, came to him, and he remembered how the man's eyes had fastened on him with hatred. At last he shoved Emas and the Dark Lord out of his mind and went to sleep. But he tossed and turned most of the night.

The next day at breakfast, Mat tasted the porridge that the girls had cooked, and a frown crossed his face. "What is this? It tastes like paste."

"It's porridge, Mat," Sarah said. She did not grow angry, for she knew that this was simply Mat's way. He seldom had anything good to say about anyone or anything. Tam, on the other hand, grinned and reached for Mat's bowl. "I'll eat it, brother, if you don't want it."

"Keep your hands to yourself, and don't be so confounded cheerful! I've got a feeling we're going to be in a terrible situation."

"Give no thought for the morrow," Josh said. "Sufficient to the day are the troubles we've got right now."

When they had finished eating and the others went outside, Josh offered to help Sarah clean up after the meal. The two of them heated water in the fireplace. Then Sarah washed the tin dishes and flatware while Josh dried them and put them in a box that was nailed to the wall.

"Remember what it was like to have a dishwasher?" he asked suddenly.

"Do I!" Sarah breathed fervently. "And I used to complain about having to wash dishes."

"We complained about a lot of things in Oldworld. Like having to walk to school instead of going in a car."

Sarah handed Josh a platter, then asked thoughtfully, "Do you think about those days a lot?"

"I do," Josh said. He dried the plate slowly. "I miss my parents."

"I miss mine, too," Sarah said. "I think about them all the time. Every day."

The two worked on until finally the dishes were done, and Sarah said, "How about a tea party?"

Josh grinned. "We used to have those when you first came to live with us. I thought they were silly."

"And you laughed at my dolls too, but you finally got to where you would play with them."

Josh glanced over his shoulder with a worried look. "Don't let that get around. If Reb ever found out I played with dolls, he'd never let me hear the last of it."

"There's nothing wrong with boys playing with dolls. Just like there's nothing wrong with girls playing baseball."

"I know. I used to play with G.I. Joes for hours on end. Remember the wars we used to have?"

"Yes, and I always had to be the enemy," Sarah said. "You would never let me be one of the good guys."

Josh looked over at Sarah. She was wearing a simple dress that came down just to her knees. It was made of some soft, pale green material. "That's a nice looking dress," he said.

"Well, things are looking up! You never used to compliment my clothes. Do you really like it?"

"Sure. It looks nice on you."

The two made tea and sat and sipped it and talked about the adventures they had had since coming to Nuworld.

"Sometimes I have bad dreams about the Dark Lord," Sarah confessed. "He frightens me."

"He frightens just about everyone. Not just us, either. Everywhere we go, people are scared stiff of him. He's got lots of strange powers."

"If it weren't for Goél, I don't think I could bear living here," Sarah said.

"I wish he'd come soon. He may send us out on some awful mission, but it'd be better than just hanging around here."

Josh did not get his wish that day, and the Sleepers spent their time hunting for squirrels. There were no guns in Nuworld, so all of them had learned to use the bow and arrow. To hit a squirrel with an arrow was quite a feat, and Sarah turned out to have the surest eye. She got three squirrels, and Reb brought down four with a slingshot that he had made of some elastic and a forked stick.

"I don't see how you hit anything with that," Jake complained. He was not a very good archer, nor was he good with a slingshot. "If I just had my .22, I'd show you what squirrel hunting was really like. I could hit anything with that gun."

Jake stood watching Reb skin the squirrels for supper. Reb was very good at it. He just made a simple cut or two, then ripped off the hide as easily as taking off a small overcoat.

"I don't see how you do that, Reb." Jake shook his head. "I'd make a mess out of it."

"If you'd cleaned as many squirrels as I have, you could do it, too."

"Do you think Goél will come pretty soon?" Jake asked suddenly.

"I reckon so."

Reb's attention was not altogether on the squirrels, and Jake had noticed. "What are you thinking about?"

"Guess I was thinking about back in Camelot. That was really my kind of place."

Their adventure in Camelot had been a high hour for Reb Jackson. The people there had somehow arrived at a civilization much like King Arthur's court. Being the best horseman of any of the Sleepers, Reb had become an expert jouster. "Someday I'm going back to Camelot," he said.

Jake did not answer right away. "I'd just like to go back home," he said finally.

"You mean back to Oldworld?"

"Yes."

"That's all gone, Jake. You might as well forget it."

"How can I forget it?" Jake said. "I'd give anything just to walk down a street again with big buildings on both sides. Go out to Coney Island, catch a movie. All the things I liked to do, they're all gone."

Reb shook his head. "I miss a lot of things, too. I don't ever get to go trot lining like I did back in Arkansas."

"We could do that here, but we can't build a city like New York again!"

Josh and the other boys watched Sarah and Abbey set about making squirrel stew for supper.

"Can you make some dumplings?" Reb asked. "Squirrel and dumplings go mighty good."

"Maybe not like your mom used to make, Reb," Abbey said, "but we'll do the best we can."

"I saved the brains. You could have some of them, Abbey. Nothing like squirrel brains for taste."

Abbey shuddered. "No, thanks!"

"You don't like squirrel brains?"

"I don't know. I've never tasted any and don't intend to."

Supper went well, though the meat was rather scarce. The squirrels did not go far, divided among ten people. Volka probably could have eaten them all himself. Instead he filled up, more or less, on the pasta that Sarah had learned to make.

When the dishes were done, they sat around talking, and then things turned rather gloomy. It wasn't long before an argument broke out between Jake and Dave Cooper. The two were just starting to shout at each other, in spite of Wash's plea to cool it, when all of a sudden the door swung open. There stood a tall figure wearing a gray robe. A hood shadowed his face, but as the man entered he pushed it back.

"Goél!" everyone cried.

Goél was a lean man, not handsome but strong-looking, and there was strength in his face and warmth in his dark eyes. He came to the center of the room, saying, "Greetings, my young friends." He glanced at Dave and Jake and smiled slightly. "I see you're still showing great love and affection for one another."

Both Dave and Jake looked terribly embarrassed. To ease the strain, Josh said quickly, "Goél, we've been waiting for you. Come and sit down. Have something to eat."

"I'm afraid there's not time for that," Goél said. He had a pleasant voice, one that the Sleepers could never mistake. It was quiet right now, but there was hidden power in it. Josh knew that at times Goél could raise his voice until it was like the roll of distant thunder.

Mat looked relieved but could not help complaining. "Well, we've been waiting for you, sire," he said. "We expected you earlier."

Goél seemed to find this amusing. He smiled. "Mat, you are always unhappy, but I do not come on command."

Somehow Mat could not meet the eyes of the tall man. He dropped his glance to the floor and muttered, "Well, we were just anxious to see why you commanded us all to meet."

"It is a fair question, Mat." He looked about the group and said, "I hope you are well rested, for I have a mission that will involve considerable effort."

Something very close to fear came over Josh. He was a shy boy, never completely certain of himself, always thinking he was a failure. And now the thought of leading this group anywhere into danger frightened him. "Are you sending us far, Goél?"

"Very far indeed. To a land that is different from anything that you have encountered in Nuworld so far."

"Where is it, sire?" Tam said. "I've traveled quite a bit."

"Have you ever been to Whiteland?"

"Whiteland?" Tam looked puzzled. "No. I've never even heard of it."

"I am not surprised. As I said, it is far from here, and I would not send you if going were not of the utmost importance." Goél looked around then, as if weighing each person. Josh felt the weight of his eyes. Once Reb had told him, "When Goél looks at us like that it's like he just comes through my eyes, crawls down into my heart, and rummages around to find out what's down there. It's downright uncomfortable."

Each of them must have felt somewhat the same. Abbey kept looking down at her hands, unable to meet Goél's eyes. Everyone knew that Goél seldom explained himself, but most of them had had times when he would come to them individually and quietly talk to them about things. "I reckon we're a pretty motley group, Goél," Jake said. "I never have understood why you chose us. We're just a bunch of kids and not very talented ones at that."

"You are as talented as you need to be, friend Jake. All of you have hidden talents." He paused for a moment, and they all waited. Then he said, "It is not the easy things that make a young man or a young woman strong. It is the hard things."

"Well, we ought to be getting strong," Reb said. "We've gone through some mighty hard things."

"Yes, you have, Reb, and you are not the same young people who came to Nuworld." There was approval in Goél's warm eyes. "But now, I have another hard thing for you, and if you are faithful and strong and brave, it will make you more into true servants of Goél."

27

"I'd guess it involves the Dark Lord again, sire."
Dave Cooper spoke up suddenly, his eyes fixed on their visitor.

"It does. His arm is long, and he has reached into a group of my friends that are in great need of help."

"This Whiteland. Where is it?" Josh asked.

"It is far to the north. It will be a hard journey for all of you. It will require all of your strength just to get there."

"But how can we find the way? Are you going to draw us a map?" Sarah asked. She'd often said she had visions of getting lost in some pathless forest, and the thought frightened her.

"I have something better than a map, but first let me tell you a little about the situation. Sit down."

They all sat except Goél. Standing before them, he spoke of the Dark Lord, who had his spies and his servants everywhere. He spoke of the House of Goél, which was small. He said, "You all know the prophecy that concerns you." Then he quoted the verse that all of them knew well:

"The House of Goél will be filled,
The earth itself will quake!
The beast will be forever still,
When Seven Sleepers wake!

"There was once a young queen," he went on to say, "who was called upon to do a very daring thing. She risked her life to save her people. It was said that she came to her kingdom for just such a time as that. And now I must tell you that you Sleepers are come to Nuworld for such a time as this. The shadow of the Dark Lord grows long. More and more fall into slavery

28

in his deadly kingdom, but the Sleepers have been awakened, and one day the power of the Dark Lord will be broken."

"Will it be soon, Goél?"

Goél smiled and said quietly, "All times are the same to me, but whether soon or far in the future, your task is to be faithful to me." Then he said, "You ask how you would find your way. I have provided a guide for you." He moved to the door and called out, "Come in, Fairmina."

Josh did not know what to expect, but he and the other Sleepers got to their feet. Even as they turned to the door, a young woman stepped through. She wore clothes made of some soft blue material that clung to her athletic figure. Long blonde hair cascaded down her back.

"This is your guide," Goél said. "Fairmina is the daughter of Denhelm, chief of the Lowami tribe in Whiteland. Her mother is Rimah, who comes from a princely race."

The girl looked around at the Seven Sleepers, and Josh thought he saw disdain in her eyes.

Then she turned to face Goél. Her back was straight. She said, with scorn in her voice, "My lord Goél, my father sent me here because we are desperately in need of help to save our people."

"I understand that, Fairmina, and I am answering your father's request. These are the Seven Sleepers." He named each Sleeper and then introduced Tam, Mat, and Volka. "This is my answer to your father's plea for help."

Fairmina, princess of Whiteland, looked over the group again. "My lord, this one may do"—she waved a hand toward Volka. "He is big enough to be of help. But

as for the others, my father sent me to get *warriors!*"
A sneer twisted her lips. "We need warriors in
Whiteland, not children!"

3

A Tough Young Lady

Josh Adams could hear the scorn in Fairmina's voice. Anger raced through him, and a hot reply leaped to his lips. But then he saw Goél's eyes watching him carefully. *He wants to see if I wait for him,* Josh thought. He knew Goél often tested the Sleepers, and he knew this was one of those times. Determined not to disappoint his leader, Josh clamped his lips together. But as he glanced around, he saw that the rest of the Sleepers were not pleased with Fairmina's words, either.

Goél waited. Silence fell over the room, and surely he could see the displeasure on the faces of the company. Turning to Princess Fairmina, he said, "You are new in the service of Goél, my daughter. You must learn submission."

Fairmina drew herself up. She was a tall girl, strongly built, and there was a fierce light in her eyes. "My father has no son, sire. You are well aware of this."

"Yes, I am."

"Since there is no prince, no one to step into my father's place when he dies, he has raised me as he would have raised a son if he had had one." She looked very proud, and her green eyes flashed. "There is no man among our people who is better with a bow than I—or with a sword, either! True, I am not as strong as some of our men, but I am quicker, and none can keep up with me on a trail. My father has given me hard training, for he knows that one day I must stand in his place, woman though I be."

Goél listened patiently to this. Then he said slowly, "I know well what your father has done and that you are indeed a princess of strength. You have honor and courage. But, my daughter, you have not much of two other qualities that every ruler must have."

Suspiciously, Fairmina asked, "And what are those, if I may ask, sire?"

"Patience and gentleness."

"But our people are perishing! We must fight for our existence! There is no time for patience, and we do not need gentleness but fierce strength in order to survive!"

Silence fell over the room again.

None of the Sleepers would have dared to answer Goél in this fashion, Josh was thinking. *She doesn't know who she's talking to! If she knew who Goél was, she would be a little bit more humble.*

Goél, however, did not seem to be disturbed. He said quietly, "You do not yet know the ways of Goél, and you are very young, my daughter. Before long you will learn that sometimes gentleness is stronger than violence. And you will learn that patience is a virtue that I highly admire." A smile touched his lips then, and his gaze went to the Sleepers. "My young friends here have learned a little about how to trust me. Is it not so?"

"Yes, Goél," Josh answered immediately. "We do trust you." He looked at Fairmina. "We may not be much in your eyes, Princess, but we are the servants of Goél. His strength is enough for us."

Fairmina stared. She did not answer him, but a look of doubt crossed her face. She turned back to Goél and said, "You know that my people are at war."

"So your father says. I have not forgotten him. He

32

and I have been friends for a long time. And your mother, Rimah, is a jewel among women."

"Then you must know that if something isn't done, the Dark Lord will have us all. We'll be helpless if we don't fight—and soon!" Again she looked doubtfully at the Sleepers. "I spoke hastily, perhaps, and I ask your pardon. But my heart is heavy when I think that even now my people may be dying, waiting for help that I was sent to bring."

"You must not trust your heart, daughter," Goél said. "Trust *me*. These young people may not look like much, but they have done battle with the Dark Lord and his servants already and have not bent." Then he amended his speech, and his eyes glowed with humor. "Well, perhaps they did bend a little, but they did not break. Is that not so, Wash?"

Now Fairmina stared at the boy. Wash, the smallest of the Sleepers, was indeed most unimpressive.

Wash smiled at her. But he said, "I know you're a princess, and I'm pretty young. But I've found out that if you trust in Goél—no matter who you are—that makes you strong where you need to be strong."

"That's right," Josh said. "Wash saved us all from a monster under the sea. He's got more courage than anybody I ever saw."

"Courage is necessary," the girl agreed. "But it takes a strong arm to pull a good bow or to handle a sword, and there are so few, Goél!"

"Strength lies not always in numbers," Goél said almost sternly. "That is another lesson you must learn. The weapons of the spirit—they are what is important."

Fairmina bowed her head, and Josh could see that she was disappointed. She murmured, "As you say, sire. I have obeyed my father."

"You are not convinced, my daughter, but I know that in the days to come you will learn many truths." He put his hands on her shoulders, and she looked up, startled. He said nothing.

The Sleepers watched, holding their breath. In the silence, Goél seemed to be telling Fairmina something, not with words but with some communication directly to her heart. Finally, he dropped his hands and turned again to the Sleepers. "It is good to see you again, my young friends. I have missed you. Now, we will sit and talk and you will tell me what is in your hearts."

"Goél is gone!"

Josh burst into the hut. He had gone looking for Goél while the others were finishing breakfast. He'd returned almost immediately. "He's not here at all! I thought he'd say good-bye, at least!"

"That's the way he is." Sarah sighed. "He comes and goes without warning." She looked over at Fairmina, who was sitting on a bench staring out the window. "Did you talk to him before he left?"

"Yes. You were all asleep." This seemed to imply some criticism.

"You sound like it's a crime to go to sleep!" Jake cried. "Well, I'm here to tell you we're just humans, Princess. We have to sleep once in a while. Perhaps you royal folks don't, but we common people do."

Fairmina gaped at the redheaded boy and then smiled. "You have spirit, Jake. I like that. You are small, but Goél said some fine things about you. You seem to be one of his favorites."

Jake flushed to the roots of his hair. "Aw . . . well . . . I'm not much," he said. "I'm not as strong as Dave here, and I can't lasso with a rope like Reb."

34

"Goél talked about all of you after you went to sleep. Now I understand a little more about his confidence in you."

Sarah looked pleased. "He always knows how to make a person feel better."

Fairmina's face suddenly grew sad. "While he was speaking, I was encouraged. But now, in the cold light of day, I truly do not see how a small number such as this can help. I expected to lead a troop of a thousand back to Whiteland to fight our enemies. Hundreds, at least."

Mat had been watching the girl's face. "That's just what I say. How can a little bunch like us do anything?"

"Will you be quiet, Mat!" Tam told him. "Goél's never sent us in the wrong direction yet!"

Josh was studying Fairmina. "I know you're not convinced yet, but I hope that you'll think better of us after a while."

"What orders did Goél leave, Fairmina?" Sarah asked.

"He orders that you follow me."

"Then you'll be our leader," Josh said, feeling some relief.

"Yes, I'll lead you to Whiteland. But once we are there, Goél said you would have to do what seems right to you." Heavily, she added, "I do not think we will succeed, but I must go back and give my life for my people."

"Just tell us what to do," Dave said.

Reb nodded. "We'll do our best."

"First of all, how do we get to Whiteland?" Josh asked. "It's a long way, isn't it?"

"Many, many long miles. But we will not walk all the way." Fairmina reached into an inner pocket and

35

pulled out a soft leather bag. When she slapped it into her other hand, it made a pleasant clinking sound. "Goél has given me gold to buy horses and pack animals. We will ride as far as we can."

"That's a relief!" Jake said. "I'm not much of a horseman, but I'd rather ride than walk. My legs aren't as long as Reb's here."

Two days later the party started out at dawn, all mounted on sturdy horses. They had purchased food, and that, along with equipment such as their swords, shields, and armor, was carried by three sturdy pack animals. The horses were small, like mountain ponies, but Reb knew horseflesh and had helped with the purchase.

He said, "These are tough animals. I wish they were Texas mustangs, but they're the closest thing to it. They'll be plodding on when some long-legged thoroughbred would give up and quit."

Tam and Mat rode a single horse. Mat sat behind, clinging to Tam's waist. No horse was big enough for Volka, but his strides were so long that he had no trouble keeping up with the horses. "Ho," he boomed, "I will have to be careful not to walk off and leave your little toy horses."

Princess Fairmina led the way, and all morning long they moved along the trail northward. It was pleasant going. When the sun was directly overhead, they stopped to eat. But after only a quick break, they proceeded again.

By the time they stopped for the night, Mat was groaning. "Get me off this horse!"

Fairmina looked at him with a frown. "A ride like

36

this, and you're ready to give up? I thought Gemini dwarfs were tougher."

Her remark squelched what spirit Mat had, and he complained even more vehemently.

The Sleepers fell into their regular routines. The boys went out to gather wood and made a fire while the girls broke out the cookware and began to put a meal together. They had fresh meat, and for once Mat did not complain but ate hungrily.

"What do you think this is?" Abbey asked. "It doesn't taste like any meat I've ever had."

Reb, who loved to tease, said, "Maybe horsemeat. Tastes kind of like it."

Abbey stared at the meat and said, "Ugh!" She was about to put it aside when Dave laughed. "Don't believe him. It's good Nuworld beef. You'd better enjoy it, for we may really be eating horsemeat before we get to where we're going."

After eating, Princess Fairmina sat off by herself. And long after the others had rolled into their blankets, she stared into the fire.

Finally she gave a sigh and pulled up her own blanket. Her last waking thought was, *I don't see what good these children are. My father and mother will be so disappointed. They think I'm bringing back an army —and I'm bringing back a nursery.*

From far away a voice came to Sarah, and then a hand shook her roughly. "Wake up. It's time to get started."

"But I just went to bed." Sarah clutched her blanket and blinked against the sun, which was barely risen in the sky.

Princess Fairmina was standing over her, an unhappy look on her face. "Are you going to sleep all day?"

"No. I'm awake. I'm getting up."

Somewhat embarrassed, Sarah jumped out of her blanket. She washed her face in the stream they had camped beside and then began frying bacon and heating bread over the campfire.

The Sleepers and their companions ate quickly and were in the saddle by seven o'clock.

The day was a repeat of the first with one exception. The Sleepers, unused to ten-hour rides, were all sore. Sarah found that the inside of her legs were chafed almost raw. Abbey had the same problem, and the two girls tried to comfort each other. "We'll toughen up," Sarah said with a confidence she did not feel.

"No, we won't. We'll probably die before we get there."

They rode hard for the next three days, and by that time all of them had gotten somewhat used to being on horseback for long stretches. Volka, of course, was as tough as an oak tree. With one smashing blow of the club he always carried, he managed to kill a huge wild hog that weighed several hundred pounds. That night they had a feast and slept better than usual.

The next day, Princess Fairmina stopped her little army while the sun was still high in the sky—which surprised everybody.

"We can go farther, Fairmina," Josh said.

"This is enough for today. There is something we have to do."

The something that Fairmina had in mind was to check out their skill with weapons.

She quickly discovered that Mat and Tam, for all their short heights, were expert swordsmen. The others seemed to have varying skills with the sword. Dave was the best. He was the strongest and had the longest reach. Fairmina nodded grudgingly after she had gone victoriously through a bout with him. "You do very well, Dave."

Dave shook his head. "I never thought I'd be bested by a woman."

"You have not crossed blades before with any woman that has practiced every day of her life since she was six years old."

She found some of them practically helpless with a sword. These included Wash and Abbey.

Finally she said, "We'll test you out with a bow."

All of them were armed with bows except for Volka, whose only weapon was his terrible club.

Finding an open place, Fairmina attached a target to a tree and then marched back some thirty paces. "Now, each one of you shoot at that mark."

Josh's heart sank. The target was a small card no bigger than a playing card. Nevertheless, he drew his bow and launched an arrow. It missed the whole tree, and Josh flushed. "I guess I'm out of practice."

"I can see that," the princess said. "Now, the rest of you."

As with the sword, there were varying skills.

Sarah loosed one arrow that hit the edge of the card, and Fairmina exclaimed, "A good shot! You are a fine archer, Sarah!"

Reb Jackson grinned. "I'm not much with one of these things. I could do better with a .44."

"What's a .44? Never mind. We don't have any here. Take your best shot, Reb."

Reb managed to hit the tree, although his arrow was two feet lower than the card.

Fairmina was not happy. "I think most of you would starve in my country. Our lives depend upon our skills with a bow. Except for Sarah, all of you are in need of practice."

The weapons session was a humiliation to the Sleepers. It was also humiliating that, except for the huge boar that Volka had killed, most of the game that they fed on was brought down by the princess. She would ride on ahead, and later they would find her with a bird or a squirrel or a rabbit.

Sarah, especially, felt humiliated. She said to Josh, "I'm going to help with the hunting."

"I wish just one of us could do something right," Josh said. "The princess doesn't think much of us."

That night, after they had eaten fried rabbit and the last of the bread they had brought with them, the boys withdrew to their section of the camp. By common consent, they gave the girls plenty of room.

Princess Fairmina sat watching Sarah and Abbey take turns brushing each other's hair.

"You spend a lot of time making yourselves look nice," she commented. She herself simply put her hair into braids and then coiled them in a crown around her head. "Why do you do it?"

"Why, I guess every girl wants to look as good as she can," Abbey said with surprise.

"You don't spend much time on your appearance, do you?" Sarah observed. "But I'll bet you have lots of boyfriends."

"What do you mean? I have friends who are boys and friends who are men and friends who are girls and friends who are women."

"No. I meant—well, suitors. Young men that come *courting* you," Sarah said.

Princess Fairmina threw a chunk of wood onto the fire and watched the sparks climb upward. There was something like sadness in her strange green eyes. "I have no time for such things," she said simply.

"But surely you want to marry someday and have children—be a wife and mother."

"I will be the chieftess of the Lowami. They will look to me to lead them forth in war. I will have no time for such things as suitors."

"But don't you want a sweetheart?" Abbey persisted. Puzzled, she studied Fairmina's face. Apparently she could not understand this young woman at all.

The fire crackled and snapped, and the smell of smoke was rich and strong.

Princess Fairmina seemed to consider Abbey's question. But then she shook her head and spread out her blanket. "I have no time for such foolishness!" she said firmly. She lay down and seemed to go to sleep instantly.

"I never saw a girl that didn't want to get married," Abbey whispered.

"I guess it's hard trying to be a son instead of a daughter. I feel sorry for her."

"Well, the way she's driving us, I feel sorry for *us*. Good night, Sarah."

"Good night, Abbey."

4

A Cold Trail

The journey seemed to go on forever. It was true that the Sleepers had toughened and could now stand daylong rides in the saddle, but the terrain was hard going. The food that they had brought along was all gone. They lived on what they could bring down with their bows. From time to time, Volka would kill a beast with his club, but it was either feast or famine.

It also was cold.

"I'm freezing to death," Abbey complained one day. They were riding along a rocky trail that led over a mountain pass. The trees were only a few scattered evergreens. It was a barren looking scene. Abbey looked around and shuddered. "I hate this country!"

Sarah took in the bleak landscape and nodded. "I don't like it either. It's not very pretty."

"Very pretty!" Abbey exclaimed. "It's hideous! I don't think we're ever going to get there, and it's so *cold!*"

They had left the sunshine behind several days ago, and the skies were lowering and gray. A moaning wind whipped around them, biting at them with its freezing breath. They had all put on their warmest clothes, but only Fairmina had fur trousers, fur-lined boots, and a hood that she could pull down over her face. The furs were white and the prettiest that any of the Sleepers had ever seen.

"I wish we all had fur coats like that," Reb managed to say through chattering teeth. "I never could stand cold weather."

"And there's snow coming," Josh predicted. He tried not to complain, but he also had been raised in the South and was not accustomed to the cold.

"Why don't you ask her how much farther it is, Josh?" Dave suggested.

"Well, it couldn't hurt. I'll see where we are." He pushed his small pony ahead until he caught up with Fairmina.

The princess turned to face him. "What is it?"

"I hate to complain, but we're not used to this cold weather, Princess."

"Cold!" Fairmina exclaimed. "You call this cold?"

"Don't you?"

She laughed. "This is not cold. You will see cold in a few days. Real cold."

"How much farther is it?"

"We will hit the ice country tomorrow. Then the pleasant part of our journey will be over."

Josh was stunned. He let his horse fall back, and the other Sleepers gathered around him.

"What did she say?" Sarah asked. "Will we be there soon?"

Josh laughed with a hollow sound. "She didn't say. She just said the fun part of our journey's almost over."

"Fun part!" Wash said. He was beating his hands together to bring some life into them. "She calls this fun?"

"She says this isn't really cold," Josh said grimly.

"Well, if this ain't cold, I'd hate to see what is," Reb said. "My Uncle Seedy, he said it got so cold one time where he lived that when he said something, the words froze. Fell right on the ground. They had to wait until spring until they thawed out so they could hear what he was saying."

Reb always was telling some tall tale like this. Usually they brought a laugh, but this time everyone was too miserable.

"Well," Dave said, "we can't turn back. And Goél wasn't joking when he said this would be a real test."

For the next three days, the weather grew colder and colder. Then, late one afternoon, Princess Fairmina reined in her horse and waited for the others to catch up. She swung an arm and said, "There is Whiteland."

They all stared, and Josh's heart sank. "It's nothing but snow and ice!"

"Of course. That is why we call it Whiteland. What did you expect?" the princess snapped.

"I don't know what I expected," Josh said. "Is it all like this?"

"There are mountains, and in the summer there is much green pasture when the snow melts. But this is not summer now. It is the worst part of winter. I myself would not have planned such a dangerous journey, for the cold can kill as easily as an arrow."

Josh had never seen such a barren landscape. *For sure we'll all die in this place*, he thought. The cold was already bitter, and his hands were so stiff he could not feel them.

Sarah said, "I don't mean to put you down, Fairmina, but this is an awful place for those of us who are used to warmer climates."

"It is a hard land, and only hardy people can live here," Fairmina admitted, "but it is my home. It is beautiful at times. You will soon see the great lights—all the colors of the rainbow all over the sky."

"That's the northern lights," Jake said with interest. But his teeth were chattering, and his shoulders jerked with the cold. "I'd like to see them. It's a nice place to visit. But I wouldn't want to live here."

"Come. We can go only a few more miles with the horses."

"We've got to leave the horses behind?" Josh said with astonishment.

"Certainly. They could not travel through the deep snow."

"You don't have any *horses* in your country?" Reb asked.

"No. We have other animals—reindeer, moose, wolves, others—but not horses. They could not survive the winters. They are not hardy enough."

"But what will we do with these horses?"

"Leave that to me," Fairmina said.

They reached a village just as the sun was going down. The place was a collection of huts and stone houses scattered over a small area, apparently without any plan or forethought. There was an inn, however, and Fairmina said, "We can stay here tonight."

"I'll be glad to get in a bed again!" Sarah sighed.

A short, dumpy man named Farroh served them a hot meal. It was not particularly well cooked. The meat was tough, and when Reb asked what it was, Farroh said shortly, "Moose."

"Well, it's not tougher than shoe leather," Reb commented. He chewed vigorously, then said, "I hope the rest of the critters in this part of the world aren't so tough."

"You can sleep late tomorrow," Fairmina told them with a tight smile. "I have business to take care of."

"Well, that's a relief!" Wash said. "I feel like I haven't slept more than an hour at a time since we started this trip." He was standing beside the fire, soaking up the heat. "I'm going to sleep right here in front of this fireplace," he said, "unless there's one in our bedroom."

The "bedrooms" were two upstairs rooms, neither of which had fireplaces. There were no beds either— simply rough mattresses. These were stuffed with some sort of seeds and were not much softer than the floor itself.

Josh stayed awake for a while, talking with Dave about the future. "I'm worried, Dave," he said. "It was all I could do just to stay on a horse in this awful cold. How can we *walk?*"

"I know what you mean," Dave said. "It's so cold outside I can't even talk. My lips get frozen."

"Fairmina doesn't seem to mind."

"She was born here. She's used to it. But the rest of us aren't that tough." He bit his lip. "I don't know, Josh. This looks like a mighty tough assignment to me."

When Josh woke up the next morning, he hated to get out from under the thin blankets. He had been cold all night. But he got up anyway and dressed quickly. "Let's go downstairs, fellas. Maybe there's a fire down there."

"Maybe they've got a good bunch of hotcakes ready for us," Reb said hopefully.

They found the girls already huddled in front of the fireplace.

"I didn't sleep a wink," Abbey said. "There was no bed, and that mattress was worse than riding a horse."

"Where'd Fairmina go?" Dave asked their host.

Farroh grunted but made no answer.

"Thanks a lot," Dave said. "I'll always appreciate that good information."

They ate breakfast—it was hot porridge—and when

Farroh complained that they ate too much, Volka put his enormous hands around the man's neck. He half lifted him off the floor and boomed, "More food! More food!"

"All right! All right! Put me down! You can have more."

Volka put the man down and proceeded to eat enormous quantities of porridge.

Just as they finished breakfast, suddenly Dave, who was looking out the window, said, "There comes Fairmina. She's driving a *dog team!*"

They all pulled on their coats and piled outside as the princess drew up the team with a spoken command.

"What beautiful dogs—and so big!" Sarah cried.

"Good sled dogs. I traded the horses for them."

"But we can't all ride in that little sled," Josh said.

Fairmina laughed. "Ride in the sled! No. That's for the supplies. Come inside. Bring those bundles with you."

The bundles proved to be fur outfits that Fairmina had bought with some of the gold that Goél had provided. "We'll be leaving soon," she said. "Put on these furs. They ought to keep you warm, and I also bought special underwear for all of you."

Up in the girls' bedroom with their bundles of fur, Sarah said, "These are *beautiful furs!* I wonder what they are."

"They look like mink. It's such soft fur, and I bet they're warm."

"And look at this!" Sarah said as she opened a package. She drew out what appeared to be long underwear and socks. "Why, they're like silk!" she marveled.

When the girls put on the underwear, they found that, whatever the material was, it had marvelous insulating qualities. "They're kind of like wet suits," Abbey decided—she had done a little snorkeling. "They keep the cold out like magic."

The fur outfits were made in three parts—trousers that were held up by a drawstring, a parka with a hood that could be pulled down about the face, and a pair of sturdy, fur-lined boots.

They were also provided with fur mittens.

The girls admired themselves, and Abbey said, "These would cost a fortune back in Oldworld. If they really *are* mink, they'd probably be ten thousand dollars apiece."

"Well, they're worth it if they'll keep us warm. Come on. Let's go see what the boys look like."

The boys were downstairs, all wearing their fur outfits. Volka looked the strangest of all.

Fairmina explained, "I had to have three suits split and resewed for him. But without them, he would freeze to death just like the rest of you."

Volka looked like a walking mountain of fur. He laughed a booming laugh and said, "Warm! Feels good!"

The rest of the morning was spent purchasing supplies. By the time the sled was loaded with their weapons and food for the journey, even Fairmina shook her head. "It will be hard work for the dogs."

"But what about us? It's snowing out there. That snow's already two feet deep. We couldn't get a hundred yards without giving out," Josh cried.

"That's what these are for." Fairmina brought out a pair of snowshoes. "I have a set for each of you. Have you ever used snowshoes before?"

No one could say yes to that, and again Fairmina

shook her head. "It will be hard for you, then. But come. I will give you your first lesson. We must get on our way. I fear for my people."

Walking on snowshoes was an entirely new experience for the Sleepers. They fastened them on, and Fairmina began instructing them. Nearly all of them took one step and fell down.

"You can't walk normally," Fairmina explained patiently. "If you move your legs straight ahead as you usually walk, one snowshoe will land on the top part of the other and hold it down. That's why you're falling."

"What do we do, then?" Josh asked in embarrassment.

"You have to spread your legs wider apart than usual and take longer steps." Fairmina demonstrated. She herself had no trouble, but it took some time to get everyone else ready to move.

"All right," she said at last. "We'll leave now. We have to make up as much time as we can, and I expect you'll be sore tomorrow."

They did not get very far that first day. The snowshoes proved to be a great problem for all except Fairmina. Time and again someone would forget to swing his legs clear, would step on the other snowshoe, and go down in the snow. Everyone's legs began to ache, and by two o'clock Abbey said, "I can't go any farther."

"I don't think I can, either," Sarah confessed. "We're just not used to this, Fairmina."

"All right. I'm not surprised. We will camp over against that rock. It will be a little shelter."

The "little shelter" was just a large cliff that leaned outward. The snow beneath it was only an inch or two deep, however.

Fairmina loosed the dogs and fed them dried fish.

She also offered to do most of the cooking, since Abbey and Sarah were exhausted.

Some wood was available, but it took a lot of searching. By the time the boys had gathered enough for a fire, they were exhausted, too. Volka wandered off and brought back an enormous dead tree and simply broke off branches with his huge club. He seemed to be enjoying himself.

Mat said, "Aren't you tired, Volka?"

"Tired! Are you?"

Mat hated to admit that he ever had any weaknesses. "No, I'm not tired!" he snapped.

"Yes, you are," Tam said wearily. "You're as tired as I am." The Gemini twins possessed the strange ability to know just how each other felt. There was also something else strange about them. They could not be separated by distance. If they got beyond a certain number of miles from each other, both began to sicken. And if they were not brought back together, they would die.

Fairmina soon had the supper ready. This time it was simply meat heated on skewers over the fire. Everyone but Volka was ready for a rest, and after eating and then drinking a little of the hot tea that they had brewed, they all fell into their blankets and went to sleep.

The next few days were torment for the Seven Sleepers. When they awoke the next morning, their legs were so sore that Abbey cried out, and the rest of them said they wanted to.

Reb massaged his legs. "I've never been so sore in my whole life," he said, "but if that woman can do it, I can too," he said grimly.

They struggled on, trying to make as much progress as they could, but it was three days before the soreness was worked out.

On that third day they were practically out of food. The trees were far more scarce now, so even firewood was hard to come by.

It was just after noon when they found themselves by what looked like a frozen sea. Fairmina suddenly halted the dog team. She quickly rummaged around in the sled and brought out what appeared to be a spear.

"What do you see? Is it an enemy?" Josh cried.

"No. A seal. Wait here. You don't know how to hunt seal."

The Sleepers watched Fairmina, in her white ermine furs, cautiously make her way toward a patch of open water. Then they saw her freeze, and Josh said, "I can't even *see* a seal."

"Well, she can, I reckon," Reb said.

Sure enough, in one smooth motion Princess Fairmina arose and cast the harpoon.

"She's got him!"

For a few moments, Fairmina struggled with the harpoon rope, hauling something dark out of the hole in the ice. Then she threw her catch over her shoulder and came back. "Not a very large one," she said, "but he'll do."

"Are seals good to eat?" Reb asked. "Don't think I've ever eaten seal. They don't have 'em where I come from."

The princess said, "They're very good." She took her knife from its sheath and cut away the soft fur. "This would make good garments, but we do not have time to cure it." The seal's blubber was white and thick. She cut off a chunk and stuffed it into her mouth.

Watching her eat the raw fat, Josh felt his stomach roll over. When she offered some to him, he said, "Is there any way to *cook* it?"

Fairmina laughed. "It's better this way. You get more strength from it. Here, you'd all better have some."

The princess got no takers, however. "You'll get tougher as you go on," she said, "but I'll cook it for you tonight."

Seal cooked over an open fire was fishy tasting, but they were hungry. After the first bite or so, Josh grew used to it.

Abbey shuddered, but she forced a bite down. "I never thought I'd eat anything like this," she said.

The next morning the Sleepers decided that seal blubber did indeed have great strengthening powers. They found they had energy to forge on, though the weather turned colder and the land they were traveling over became mostly ice.

Two days after Fairmina killed the seal, Reb killed a bear. He spotted it, grabbed the harpoon out of the sled, and charged across the ice. He had gotten to be fairly good on snowshoes.

But when he got to the bear, it reared up. It was a frightening looking creature with a red mouth and beady, evil eyes.

Reb leaped forward and threw the harpoon. It was good that he struck a hard blow, for the wounded bear took one swipe at him and knocked him head over heels.

Fairmina rushed in then with another harpoon. The bear fell full length and lay still.

"You were very foolish! This is only a half-grown bear, but he was big enough to kill you!"

"Are you all right, Reb?" Sarah asked anxiously.

"Well, he tore my coat a little, but I guess we'll have bear meat tonight. Nothing like fresh bear meat."

"You have eaten bear? You have those in your country?" Fairmina asked.

"Not white ones like this. Brown bears and black bears. Make good eating, too."

It took the rest of the day to dress out the bear and gather firewood, but they ate roasted bear meat that night. It was tough and had a very wild flavor. However, everyone decided it was better than seal.

"I suppose you're proud of yourself for having killed that bear," Fairmina said to Reb as they all sat around the fire.

"Well, I wasn't too bad, was I, Princess?" He grinned.

Fairmina studied him, and something like approval came into her eyes. "You did well," she said, "but be glad it was not an ice wraith."

Everyone looked at the princess as though something in her voice frightened them.

"What's an *ice wraith*?" Josh asked.

Princess Fairmina did not immediately answer. She just shook her head. "You will see one day, and you will not like it. Ice wraiths are evil creatures."

That night Josh dreamed of evil creatures. He never could remember his dream exactly. All he knew was that he woke up in a cold sweat, frightened to death of that thing that Princess Fairmina had called an ice wraith.

5
A Frightening Vision

"There is my home."

Princess Fairmina pulled up the dog team and waited until the others caught up with her. They paused, and she swept her arm toward a group of round structures. Smoke was rising from most of them.

"Why, they're igloos!" Josh exclaimed.

"Igloos? I do not know igloos," Fairmina said with a puzzled frown. "Those are our houses." She spoke to the dogs then, and they leaped forward.

The Sleepers followed as best they could. They could not make as good time as the dogs could.

As soon as they came into the village, they were surrounded by the Lowami people. Most of them had their hoods back, and Josh saw that they had fair hair. Many had blue eyes. *They don't look like Eskimos,* he thought. *They look like people that came from the South, with hair and eyes like that.*

"My father, this is Josh—who is the chief among the Seven Sleepers. This is my father, Denhelm."

Denhelm, Josh saw, was a tall, blond man. His skin was burned by the northern sun and weathered. Though he was not old, his face was lined.

"You are welcome to the land of the Lowami," he said, using the common language of Nuworld that was understood almost everywhere.

"Thank you, Chief Denhelm," Josh said quickly. "Let me introduce my companions." He named off the Sleepers, then introduced Mat and Tam and Volka.

"You are all welcome," Denhelm said. "This is my wife, Rimah, and later you will meet the members of my council. But now you are weary from your long journey. You will sleep tonight in the Long House."

The Long House was the one structure in the village that was indeed long and was built of stone. The doorway was very low, and the tallest of the Sleepers had to bow as they went in. The roof was made of saplings covered with furs. The interior was illuminated by three long, slitted windows, burning oil lamps, and two fireplaces. It was relatively warm inside.

"This is where you will stay temporarily. I hope you will find it comfortable," Chief Denhelm said courteously.

"You are very gracious, Chief," Josh said. "Indeed, we are tired."

"It has been a long journey for you. First you will eat, and then you will rest."

That sounded good to Josh and probably to everyone else. Hot food was brought into the Long House— a stew of some kind, which they ate hungrily.

After they had eaten, Princess Fairmina said, "Now you will sleep. There is no need to rise until you are rested."

"Well," Josh said, when they were alone in the Long House, "we're here anyway."

Looking about him, Jake said, "I've seen pictures of places like this. The Indians in Canada used to have them."

"This is a whole lot like the Arctic. Ice and snow," Dave said. "I guess the people live on fish and seals and whales just like the old Eskimos did."

"Maybe they are descendants from the Eskimos," Josh said. "Except that Eskimos had dark eyes, and most of these people have blue eyes. I don't understand that."

They sat around talking for a while, then wrapped

themselves in the furs that served for blankets. They were all exhausted. The girls took one end of the hut, and the boys the other with a fur curtain drawn between. The fire in each section burned with a feeble flame, but after their having slept outside, the Long House seemed warm and comfortable.

"I suppose everything's relative," Jake muttered to Wash, who was on his right.

"What do you mean?"

"I mean, it must be close to freezing inside here. We'd be shaking and shivering if we hadn't been toughened up on the trail. Why, it actually feels warm!"

"It does!" Dave said, who was on the other side of Jake. "As a matter of fact, I may have to throw the furs back."

On the other side of the curtain, the girls were comfortably bundled up.

"It feels so good to be out of the wind and the cold!" Abbey exclaimed. "And having hot stew. That was so good. I'm grateful for this place. I've had enough of the open trail."

"The people seem friendly, too," Sarah said sleepily. The hot food and the warmth and the fire were affecting her. "I can't stay awake any longer," she moaned. "I may sleep for a week."

Everyone in the Long House slept for nearly twenty hours. When they finally all got up and stepped outside, they saw the chief talking with his daughter.

"Good morning," Chief Denhelm said. "I trust you slept well."

"Very well, indeed!" Josh told him. "The Long House is very comfortable."

"Today, if you feel strong enough, we will show you how to make your own houses."

"You mean igloos?"

"Igloos. Is that what you call our houses?" the chief asked.

"That's what people used to call them back where we came from, although we didn't actually have any igloos ourselves."

"We simply call them houses. After breakfast, we will begin work."

They were fed a good, warm breakfast of some kind of porridge. Then the Sleepers, Tam, Mat, and Volka were led to a snow-covered field. Chief Denhelm gave them long knives, almost like swords. "It is not difficult to make a house of snow." He smiled suddenly. "If you've done it many times, ever since you were a boy."

The snow was heavy and hung together well when the chief carefully cut out a block. He said, "Here is the first block. Daughter, show them how to trim the edges." Then he cut another and handed it to Jake.

Jake was highly interested. He watched closely as the princess carried the first block to a circle she had marked out on the ground.

She set it on the inside of the circle and then took Jake's block. "You see, with these knives you must carve and angle the snow blocks so that the two meet tightly together. It must be a very good fit."

He watched her shave off the sides of both blocks until they fit perfectly.

"I see what you mean. Each one of them is a little bit thinner at the back."

"Exactly. Now, we make one circle all the way around."

The Sleepers found the building of an igloo a fascinating experience. Soon they had completed one circle of snow blocks.

"Where's the door?" Jake wanted to know.

"It's easier to cut it later. Now we will do the second layer. This time we not only have to cut the sides but the bottom of each one, too—so that the second row will be tilted in just a little."

"I get it," Jake said. "And we cut each row a little bit more off the bottom so that it tilts in more."

"It gets very difficult toward the top. If each block of snow is not frozen to those on each side of it, it will collapse."

All of them worked hard on the igloo, and although the Sleepers were awkward at it they soon learned to cut blocks of approximately the same size. Chief Denhelm and Fairmina did most of the shaping.

They stopped once to eat cold meat, but by afternoon the first igloo was about finished. It was difficult to finish the top, for that had to be done from the inside. But finally the last block was made, shaved on every side. A hole about a foot across was left in the top. Denhelm said, "That gives the smoke a way to get out."

"Just like building a fireplace," Jake said.

"Now we will make the door."

Fairmina cut an opening only two and one-half feet high, and then blocks of ice made a short tunnel to it. "That's to keep the wind out," she said. "Now, this is your house, Sarah and Abbey. We will make houses for the men next."

"Let's see what it looks like," Sarah cried.

The two girls and Fairmina went inside, and the small hole above admitted light.

"It's kind of like living inside half of an egg."

"Do we sleep on the ice?" Abbey asked.

"No," Fairmina said, "we'll put straw down and cover it with skins. Also we will build a small fireplace of rocks."

"Won't the fire melt the house?" Sarah asked with alarm.

Fairmina smiled. "No, it is so cold outside that a little fire on the inside will not melt your house."

The next two days were pleasant for the Sleepers and their friends. They built two more snow houses so that the boys could have a place to themselves. Mat and Tam and Volka shared a third. Their door had to be bigger, and even then Volka had to enter by lying flat on his stomach and crawling.

Finally the houses were finished, the straw and fur floors were put in, the fireplaces were built, and they had a celebration lighting a fire in each one. It was a little smoky, but when the fire was bright enough, the smoke curled upward and found its way outside through the opening.

"It's like camping out," Josh said to Sarah. "You girls are pretty snug, aren't you?"

"More than I thought we could be in an ice house! I never thought I'd be doing this, Josh."

"Neither did I. We've done a lot of things in Nuworld that we never thought we'd do."

One night there was a banquet, and all that could be crowded into the Long House were present. Chief Denhelm, his wife, and Fairmina sat at one end of a long line of elders. There were no tables, but the skins they sat on and the padding of straw was not uncomfortable. Women kept bringing in food.

After a while Fairmina said to Abbey, "How do you like this stew?"

"It's very good. What is it?"

"Oh, it's mostly of what you would call deer." She shrugged, then and said, "And, of course, a dog or two."

Abbey's eyes flew open, and her hand covered her mouth. She started to jump up.

But Sarah jerked her back by her parka. "Don't say anything!" she hissed in her ear. "Be polite!"

"But I can't eat dogs."

"It won't kill you. It's probably just a little bit of dog, anyway." She herself was feeling a bit queasy, but she had learned in their travels to eat what was put before her.

After the meal, they were served a drink that was much like tea. When Josh asked what it was, Fairmina said, "The plant is grown far from here, and we take the leaves. We crush them and boil them in water."

"Tastes a little bit like sassafras tea," Reb said. "Real good, Princess."

They drank tea, and the Sleepers and their friends listened as the elders talked on. One of them, a younger man, told of how he had killed a large bear. He acted it out, and his story sounded almost like poetry.

"I guess that's what they have instead of books," Josh whispered to Sarah. "It's kind of vocal history."

Then Chief Denhelm stood up. He called for attention, and everyone fell silent in respect for him. "We welcome the visitors that have been sent by Goél to help us in our battles. Perhaps they have some questions they would like to ask."

Josh said, "I guess we'd like to know a little bit more about the problem, if you wouldn't mind telling us, Chief."

Chief Denhelm was slow to answer. Then he said, "Our enemy are called the Yanti. We were once united as one tribe many years ago. But for some reason, war came, and the tribe divided."

"What was the war about?" Dave asked quietly.

"No one remembers now. But it was a sad day. Ever since then, the Lowami and the Yanti have been fighting each other."

"Are they very much like your people, Chief Denhelm?" Sarah asked.

"The tribes have been separated for many years. They are a darker people than we, with darker eyes and darker hair. Much like yours, Sarah."

"Has anyone ever tried to bring peace?"

"I have tried many times, but Balog is a warlike man."

"Is he the chief of the Yanti?" Wash asked.

"Yes. A very powerful man, and he hates our people."

"His wife does not hate us," Princess Fairmina said.

"That is true. Olah is a good woman, but she came from our tribe, you remember." He turned to Josh. "She was taken in war from our people, and Balog took her for his mate. She was a very good young woman."

"We grew up together," Rimah said. "I think if the men would get out of the way and let the women settle it, the two tribes could live in peace."

Laughter went up at this, and one of the elders said, "Next, your wife will want to be chief."

But Rimah said, "No. That is not true."

Denhelm went on explaining how the division of the tribes had brought war. "Many have been killed. It is not good."

"Then, is that why you sent to Goél, Chief? To stop the war?"

"It is, but I would not have sent if it had not been for the Ancient One." He nodded toward a very old man,

62

who had sat silently through the meal. The Sleepers were never to learn his name. He was simply called the Old One or the Ancient One. It appeared he was a priest, and everyone showed him the utmost respect.

"Oh, Ancient One, tell our guests of your vision." The old man rocked back and forth. It seemed he would never speak. His voice was thin and reedy when it came, but it grew clearer as he spoke.

"From time to time I have dreams. This one was sent from Goél, I believe."

He fell silent again, and everyone waited. Josh was impressed at the reverence the Lowami had for their priest.

"In my dream I saw terrible things. It was all in a swirling mist, but terrible beasts came and attacked our people. Many died. I grew afraid, and then I heard a voice saying, 'You must have help. Send to Goél. Ask him to send those who will help your people.'" The Ancient One stirred. "I then told my vision to the chief."

"And I sent Fairmina to find Goél and ask for help."

Fairmina started to say something but then did not.

Josh thought he knew what she was thinking. "I know you are disappointed, Chief," he said. "You were expecting Goél to send a large army, and instead you have seven very young people, two dwarfs, and a giant."

Denhelm straightened his back. His face was stern, and he said confidently, "Goél is wise. I have served him for many years. Indeed, I did look for an army, but Goél's ways are past finding out."

Suddenly the Ancient One said in a clear, strong voice,

"The House of Goél will be filled,
The earth itself will quake!

63

The beast will be forever still,
When Seven Sleepers wake!"

The words hung in the air, and with that the meeting appeared to be over. The elders got up and left. The Sleepers bowed before Rimah, who had supervised the dinner.

"It was a fine meal, Queen Rimah," Reb said.

She took their thanks, and then Fairmina was approached by Jake.

"You almost told your father that we weren't much, didn't you, Princess?"

Fairmina suddenly smiled, although she looked troubled. "Yes, I almost did. But he has always believed in the wisdom of Goél."

"Have you ever met Goél? Before this trip, I mean," Josh asked.

"Oh, yes! He has been to our village many times."

Josh was puzzled. "He's everywhere!" he exclaimed. "I don't see how he gets around so much."

"I think there is more to Goél than you and I will ever know. In any case, my friend Josh, I am glad that you have come. We need help, and you are the help that Goél has chosen. So, welcome to Whiteland."

Josh felt pleased that they had been accepted by this strong woman who could fight as well as any man. He bowed to her and returned to the igloo that he shared with Dave and Jake. They were all filled with warm food and sat talking for some time.

Josh did not take part in much of the conversation. He was listening, but he was thinking, *Fairmina is kind, but actually we do need an army. If there's going to be a war, there aren't enough of us to be of much help.*

6
The Ice Wraith

The Sleepers fell into the patterns of the Lowami tribe with little difficulty. The trip from the south had hardened them, and they found that they could bear the cold much easier now. Their warm, insulated underwear and furs made a big difference, but they knew also that the fatty food they were eating was building up their strength and their resistance to the cold.

From time to time the snows came. Then they would huddle in their small houses or else in the Long House. They learned to admire the spirit and the kindness of the Lowami people. Chief Denhelm was a man of great natural courtesy. His wife had a spirit that was quiet and gentle. The villagers, with few exceptions, were friendly, and as the days passed they found themselves liking their hosts very much.

A boy named Conmor had grown especially close to the Sleepers. He was a bright young fellow, short and muscular, very strong, and also very curious. He could never get enough stories of what Oldworld was like, and he plied the Sleepers with questions constantly.

Early one sunshiny morning, Conmor announced to the Sleepers, "We're going hunting. The meat is getting low. You are invited to join."

"Hey, that's cool, Conmor!"

"Cool?" Conmor looked puzzled. "Yes, it is cool. You would think it cold, I suppose. But why do you tell me that?"

"Oh, it's just something we say." Josh laughed. "That means it's nice—it's good—that we can go hunting with you."

Conmor's white teeth flashed against his dark, tanned skin. "I see. So when you like something, you say it's cool."

"That's right."

"Good. I will say that, too," Conmor said. "Yes. It's cool to go hunting. I will show you your weapons."

"What are we going to hunt?" Dave asked as they walked to where the hunters were gathering.

"Something to eat."

Wash laughed. "I guess that answers your question. Anything that we kill we eat."

"Why, of course," Conmor said with surprise. "Why else would we kill something if not to eat it—except one of the Yanti, of course."

"You think we'll run into any Yanti?" Jake asked.

"I do not think so. We will not be going into their territory."

The chief was going on the hunt. So was his daughter. Everyone had donned white furs, which camouflaged them against the snow.

"I guess those white furs make it easier for us to sneak up on seals or something."

"Yes, and sometimes we can harpoon a whale. They come in quite close. But I do not expect any today. We will try for a walrus. Have you ever eaten walrus?"

"Nope," Reb said. "I've eaten lizards, though."

"A walrus is not much like a lizard, but they are fat and give much strength."

The hunters started out, waving at the women as they left.

Josh was pleased to find he could do much better on his snowshoes now. He was also surprised to see that the land was not as barren as they'd first thought. Although it was winter, small clumps of trees were still green. They passed herds of reindeer that were scraping the snow away, looking for food.

"Why, there's still green grass down there!" Reb exclaimed. "You wouldn't think it would be green this time of the year under that snow."

"It is especially beautiful here in the summer. Then everything is green—the trees, the grass. I hope you will be here to see it," Fairmina said.

Secretly Josh was hoping that their quest would be over by then, but he had learned not to try to guess what would happen on any mission.

The hunters did not find any walrus after all, but under the skillful direction of Fairmina they located another herd of reindeer. They were a strain not familiar to Josh, very large, and it took considerable skill to sneak up on them.

But after a long stalk, the hunters rose up and let fly their arrows. Sarah's arrow took down one large specimen.

"Well shot, my daughter," Denhelm said. "You use a bow well."

When they'd brought down the meat supply they needed, Denhelm said, "Now, the fun is over, and the work begins."

"What is that, Chief?" Josh asked.

"We must get these animals back to camp. They will feed us for many days."

"Aren't you going to dress them out and leave the hides here?"

"Leave the hides here!" the chief cried. "That would

be waste indeed. We use all of the animals, even the antlers and bones. You will see."

Getting the large beasts back was hard work. The hunters first made three sleds of saplings and loaded the animals on them with great effort. Then, using leather thongs, they made themselves the beasts of burden to drag the heavy reindeer over the snow.

"Now I know how those sled dogs feel," Reb complained. He leaned forward against his harness and looked back to see the sled moving slowly after them. "This better be good to eat. They are sure hard to come by."

By the time they had traveled for two hours, Josh —and probably the rest of the Sleepers—was close to being exhausted. And then Volka, who was pulling one sled easily by himself, suddenly let out a yelp. Looking up, Josh saw an arrow in the giant's shoulder.

At that exact moment Fairmina cried, "The Yanti! The Yanti!"

Instantly the hunters threw down their harness and scrambled for weapons. Suddenly the air was filled with arrows.

The Yanti had taken refuge behind a slight hill, but Fairmina and her father proved to be excellent tacticians.

"You take the right, daughter. I will take the left. The rest of you hold the center."

Fairmina called out several names, Josh's among them, and these ran to the right.

"We will come up beside them on the right, and my father will lead his band to the other side," Fairmina said. "Those in front will keep them distracted. Have your arrows ready."

Josh was stumbling to keep up when they came

68

upon the enemy. Taken totally by surprise, the Yanti let out yells of fear. They turned and fled, leaving one fallen Yanti behind.

"Shall we chase them, Father?" Fairmina cried, as Denhelm appeared with his party.

"No. They are fresh, and we are weary. Let us see to our wounded and get the food back to camp."

Fairmina stood a moment over the fallen Yanti and looked sad. "There will be an empty place at their table tonight."

"But they started it," Reb said.

"I know, but this one is dead. Now his mate and his children will have no provider."

It was a side of Princess Fairmina that Josh had not seen before.

"She's really got a tender heart under that tough way of hers," Dave said. "I didn't know that."

"I did," Sarah said unexpectedly. "She talked about it one day. She really hates killing. But she has to do it because she'll be the new chief."

"Well, I guess a war leader has to be tough, all right," Jake said, "but I hate for it to be a nice young lady. Too bad the chief didn't have a son to take over when he gets too old."

None of their number had been killed, but several were wounded. One man was placed on Volka's sled. And Volka, whose injury was just a scratch to him, pulled the extra load easily.

"I guess that's enough adventure for us for one day," Josh said. His nerves were still jangled from the battle. He turned to Sarah who was pulling at the harness beside him. "Were you frightened?"

"Yes, I was. And, besides, I hate to shoot at another human being."

Josh wanted to ask if she had shot the arrow that had killed the Yanti, but he saw that she felt very bad. He had the suspicion that she had, so he said, "It was something we had to do."

"I guess so, but I hate it."

Not more than five minutes later, a scream went up from one of the Lowami warriors who was in the front.

"What is it? What's he seen? More Yanti?" Wash yelled.

They did not have to wonder long, for those in the front began falling back, all shouting something.

Fairmina suddenly was beside Josh. Her eyes glittered with hatred.

"It is an ice wraith. And we cannot flee and leave our wounded. We must fight it."

The very name *ice wraith* seemed to go through to Josh's bones, freezing them more than the cold weather. He had heard rumors about ice wraiths, but the Lowami feared them so much that they could not even clearly describe them.

Chief Denhelm was getting his warriors in order. "Archers in the second line! Spearmen in the first line! You archers, try to wound him!"

"A spearman has little chance against an ice wraith," Fairmina said, her face tense. She notched an arrow to her bow and said, "You shoot a good bow, my Sarah. Get as many as you can into the wraith."

Josh swallowed hard and stared ahead. He still could see nothing, but then suddenly a movement caught his eye.

"There he is! Archers ready!" Fairmina called out.

The line of archers drew their bows. The others

held harpoons and spears at the ready. All crouched, waiting. And then Josh saw the ice wraith.

It was a terrifying beast. It loomed enormous, as it burst out of a grove of trees. It stood upright, and Josh's first thought was, *It looks like a T-rex.*

Indeed the wraith did walk on huge hind legs, but, unlike the T-rex, it had huge forearms. And it was entirely covered with a growth of smoky white fur. The creature even looked like smoke as it swept across the snow. He understood why it was called a "wraith."

The most frightening thing was not the size or the saberlike claws, but the mouth full of teeth. Josh stood frozen with fear. *One bite of those teeth, and a human being would have no chance.* He had heard stories whispered that an ice wraith could bite a saber-toothed tiger in two with one snap of his jaws.

"Stand fast, archers! Wait until I give the word!" Fairmina's voice came clear. She seemed to have no fear. Her eyes were fixed on the ferocious beast that approached them. It moved not like a T-rex but swiftly, like an enormous weasel. The eyes were red and small and filled with evil.

"Fire!" Fairmina cried and loosed her arrow. Beside Josh, Sarah let her arrow fly. It went true, but the wraith had a tough hide. It screamed with rage in a horrible voice and kept coming.

"Again! Keep firing!" Fairmina ordered.

The wraith would make a rush. Then an arrow would manage to catch it, and it would scream like nothing that Josh had ever heard before. Its eyes flashed like fire, and only the constant rain of arrows kept its attention from the spearmen.

The Sleepers were all using their bows. Chief Denhelm was leading the spearmen. More than once

Josh thought the chief would be caught by the monster's slashing tail or by the swordlike claws on its strong forearms. The great teeth once just missed Denhelm, and Josh's heart came up into his throat.

"I've got only three more arrows, Princess," someone called.

"Make them count," she said. "When they are gone, we will have to join the men with spears."

But the ice wraith had apparently absorbed enough punishment. Giving a final scream, the monster backed away. Conmor rushed in to plant a spear in its breast, but he moved too slowly. The wounded wraith turned on him, and the hunter was suddenly inside its jaws.

"Conmor!" Reb screamed. "It's killed Conmor!"

Reb grabbed up a spear and would have run after the wraith, now retreating with its victim.

But the chief caught him and held him with his strong arms. "No, my Reb. It is too late to help him. You would be slain, too."

"We've *got* to kill it! Let me go, chief!" Reb raged.

"No," Fairmina said. She took hold of Reb's free arm. "To kill an ice wraith is something that is not easily done. Only two have ever been slain by our tribe—and then at a tremendous cost."

Reb hung his head and dropped his lance. "He was such a fine guy."

"Yes," Fairmina said sadly. "He was a fine warrior."

Now the chief rested a hand on Reb's shoulder. "We will all miss him," he said, "but you fought valiantly. All of you did." He sighed. "Ice wraiths are more cruel and more deadly than the Yanti. Come. Now we must get our wounded home."

7

The Servant of Darkness

Balog, chief of the Yantis, did not have the noble look of Denhelm, the Lowami chieftain. Balog was short, squat, and powerful. He had long, stringy black hair that sometimes hung down over his dark eyes. There was something proud and angry in his expression. He was obviously a man of a quick temper.

Seated on the fur-covered floor with his war council, Balog suddenly struck the ground beside him with a hard fist. "So the Yanti ran away!" he yelled. "That's the kind of cowards I have to put up with!"

"But, Chief," one of the council members said, "we were outnumbered." The particular speaker was pale and had a bandage around his head. He had been one of those caught in the skirmish against Denhelm's hunting party. His voice trembled a little. He probably knew the wrath of Balog could be deadly.

"Silence!" Balog shouted. "You ran away, and only cowards run away!"

Olah, the wife of Balog, had long light hair, neatly tied behind her. She had dark blue eyes, and there was a gentle spirit about her. She ordinarily took no part in the council. But now, as she brought in food, she said quietly, "Balog, sometimes even the most valiant warrior has to retreat."

He had captured Olah in a war raid against the Lowamis and, to the surprise of everyone in the tribe, had taken her as his mate instead of one of the Yanti women. If Balog had any gentleness in him at all, it was directed toward his wife. Now, however, he said impatiently, "You do not understand these things, Olah. These are matters that warriors must decide."

Seated at Balog's right was his father, Magon. He was old now, but in his day he had been a fabled warrior. No one could stand before him, and the songs of the tribe included many sagas of Magon's battles against the enemies of the Yanti. He had passed along his chief's office to his son some years ago when he was grievously wounded in battle and was unable to go out anymore. He rarely spoke in council. But when he did, everyone listened, for it was well known that Magon never gave bad advice.

"My son, there is truth in what your mate says."

Balog respected his father, although the two did not always agree.

"But, Father," he complained, "they ran away!"

"I ran away more than once in my day as war chieftain."

"Impossible!" Balog said. "I cannot believe it!"

"If I had not run away when the odds were overwhelming, there would not have been another day to fight. From what I understand of Dakar's news, they were badly outnumbered. As a matter of fact, they were foolish to attack such a large group."

Dakar nodded eagerly. "I see that now, sire. That was my mistake."

"Denhelm is a valiant warrior, and his daughter, Fairmina, is the equal of most men," his father said. "I think no shame has attached itself to our warriors."

Balog wanted to argue, but truly he had great respect for his father.

"May I say a word?"

Balog turned to the one stranger in their midst. He

knew him. He had spotted him as soon as he had seated himself. The visitor was shrouded from head to foot in a black cloak. The hood shadowed his face, but his voice came clear.

The chief shifted uneasily. "We have a guest," he said rather grudgingly. "You have heard of him. This is Zarkof, sometimes known as the pale wizard."

A murmur went around the council, for all had heard of Zarkof. It was known that he had strange powers and was closely allied with the Dark Lord himself. His stronghold had never been taken, and, although there were some rather terrible tales told about the pale wizard, none dared speak of them to his face.

"I am a self-invited guest, Chief Balog. But if I might say one word, I may be of some help to you and to the Yanti people."

Balog's eyes ran around the council. He saw apprehension in some eyes, curiosity in others. Taking a deep breath, he nodded. "We will always hear our guests, Zarkof."

"Thank you, Chief Balog." Throwing the hood back, Zarkof revealed his face. It was a sharp-featured face with deep-set, murky eyes. The color was impossible to tell. Unlike the others, who were tanned and weatherbeaten by the elements, Zarkof's face was as smooth as old marble. He had an aristocratic look and something of cruelty as well, although now he spoke gently and politely.

"Those of us in Whiteland live on the edge of the great world," he said. His voice took on a magnetic quality, almost hypnotic. Though it was not a loud voice, power was in it as he continued. "There are great things afoot in the world today. The struggle that began some years ago is reaching its climax. All of the opponents of the Dark Lord have been vanquished except for a few ragtag followers of that fellow they call Goél."

At this word, Balog saw his father narrow his eyes.

Magon said nothing, but his gaze locked with that of Zarkof, and for a moment the two seemed to be engaged in some sort of struggle. It was an emotional and a spiritual clash of wills. More than Balog must have noticed that it was Magon that Zarkof seemed to challenge rather than the chief himself.

"What is your interest in our people?" Magon asked steadily.

"To provide help. It is time for the Yanti to take their place in the sun. Why should you sit here half frozen, fighting with the other tribes for a bit of territory, when, with the help of my friend the Dark Lord, you could rule all of Whiteland."

An excited murmur ran around the council.

This, Balog well knew, was exactly what most of them desired. He slammed the floor with his fist again. "If we could defeat those blasted Lowami, then no one would stand in our way!"

"That should not be too much trouble, Chief. If you will agree to my proposals and join your forces to those of the Dark Lord, you will see that the Lowami will offer little resistance."

Zarkof talked on for some time, but then he shrugged. "But you will need to discuss this. I will leave your council. You may call me back to give me your decision."

Every eye watched as Zarkof left. At once an argument broke out. Everyone tried to talk at once. Finally Balog shouted, "Quiet! You sound like a flock of gabbling geese!"

76

One of the younger members of the council said, "Sire, it is good that we join ourselves with this man. He promises us power to defeat our enemies."

But Magon spoke up. "My son, Zarkof's words are fair, but fair words are one thing, and fair deeds are another."

"Do you find fault with him, then? Speak it out, Father," Balog said.

"In truth, there is much secrecy concerning this man. He surrounds himself with those I would not trust. It is whispered that he has many people enslaved in his fortress carved into the mountain of ice."

"Rumors," Balog said. "Just rumors. There is no proof of that."

For some time the argument raged.

"The Dark Lord, my son, is not for our people," Magon said. "He promises freedom, but I have not heard that those he rules over have it."

Balog hesitated. Rarely did he overrule his father, but finally he shook his head. "In this case, I believe we will at least listen to the man's proposal." He nodded to a servant standing beside the door. "Ask the wizard to come in."

As soon as Zarkof stepped inside, he looked around the room, his gaze searching. He must have seen the resistance on the face of Magon and the other older men of the council, but he smiled when Balog said, "We will hear more of what you would do for us, wizard."

"Gladly. You have struggled with your war against the Lowami for years now. It sways back and forth. Sometimes you win; sometimes they are the victors. What you need is something to tip the scale so that, once and for all, you can overcome them."

"Exactly! And what do you offer?"

"A weapon that will never fail." The cold eyes of Zarkof glittered. "You will rule the Lowami soon, for the weapon that I offer you neither they nor anyone else can stand against."

Again, excited murmurs went around the table.

Olah, who had been serving, came to kneel beside her husband. She put a hand on his shoulder and whispered, "Husband, this man is evil. He will bring grief to all our house."

But Balog shook her off. "Woman, this is men's work! Tend to the food!"

Then the chief rose to his feet. "Very well. As a token of good faith, you will give us a weapon. If it is successful, we will heed your words concerning the Dark Lord."

Zarkof laughed, and something—perhaps triumph?—flickered in his cold eyes. "You and your son will come with me. I will show you the power that I have."

Beorn, the son of Balog, was tall like his mother. He was so young that he was not actually on the council. So far he had said nothing. He had watched and listened carefully as the council rolled on. Now he whispered to Magon, "I wish you would go along, Grandfather. I am not sure about all this."

"Keep your eyes open as you go with this man. He is dangerous, and I'm afraid your father is easily swayed."

The following day, Zarkof, Balog, and Beorn flew over the surface of the snow in a sleigh pulled by oversized reindeer. They wound their way deep into the mountains of ice that ringed the flatlands. And then Zarkof waved a hand toward cliffs that rose high.

"Thus you see the palace of the pale wizard."

The cliffs were marked with barred windows. At the top glittered a structure that caught the sun. It had walls like white marble, and Balog gasped. "I have never seen anything like it, wizard!"

"It is my palace and my fortress. As you see, it is surrounded by steep walls that cannot be scaled. There is only one entrance, and it is guarded day and night. I do not invite many into my fortress, but since we are to be friends and companions serving under the same master, I think it is well that you see his strength."

They entered through the single gate, which rose into a recess with a clanging sound. Beorn said nothing as he walked along behind his father and the wizard. He did not trust Zarkof, but he was impressed by the strength of the man's fortress.

Guards were everywhere, heavily armored and with swords drawn. Each wore a medallion around his neck bearing the same symbol that Zarkof wore around his, except that theirs were silver and his was gold. Beorn could not see clearly what was on the medallions, but he was sure that it was a symbol chosen by the Dark Lord.

"First, Chief Balog, I will give you a tour of the palace so that you can see the magnificence you are joining yourself to."

His palace was indeed a magnificent structure. It was carved out of the mountain, and there were corridors that turned and twisted into the depths. These were illuminated by both torches and glowing stones that gave off faint light. The strange lighting gave the place a ghostly atmosphere.

The wizard took them all the way to the top, where they viewed his opulent and magnificent private

79

quarters. Everything was gold and ivory and silver. It was wealth beyond Beorn's imagination.

"And what do you think of my palace?"

"I have never seen anything like it," Balog grunted. "It would be hard to take such a place."

"Hard, indeed. Impossible. I have one more thing to show you."

He led Beorn and his father down a winding staircase, passing by windows that admitted light. Guards stood at every window, and the lifelessness in their eyes disturbed Beorn.

"Father, have you noticed the faces of the guards?" he whispered. "They're like dead men."

Balog waved his son off. "They're not our servants to worry about. This man is strong. Just come. We must see everything."

When they reached the lowest level, a huge gate made of heavy black iron barred their way.

Zarkof said, "You will now see the source of my power." He unbarred the gate and pushed it inward. Then he stepped into the passage beyond, followed by his two guests.

It was a large passageway, at least ten feet high and that wide or more. It was carved out of solid stone. It appeared to be old.

"This must have been the work of many generations ago," Beorn said.

"Yes. I inherited it. It was dug long ago by others."

The wizard suddenly halted and grew rigid. "Careful. We are in some danger here."

Both Beorn and his father stood dead still, and then Beorn gasped again— this time from fright. In the passage ahead loomed a terrifying monstrous shape. He had seen bears and tigers and white saber-toothed tigers and killer whales and ice wraiths, but nothing like this.

"What is it?" he whispered.

"That is Shivea."

The monster was in the shape of a great spider. Powerful legs rose up over her head. At the end of each leg was a cruel claw. Her eyes were multifaceted and glowing, as though there was light behind them. Venom dripped from her fangs as she sidled toward them.

But Zarkof held out the medallion that hung from his neck, and with relief Beorn saw the creature back away and slowly disappear into the gloom of a side cavern.

"Anyone who got this far would have to deal with Shivea. No trespasser has yet gotten past her."

The wizard then led his guests down a series of twisting passageways. Beorn was still shaken, but for some reason he memorized the turns. He had no thought about what he would do with such information, but he was that kind of young man. He loved knowledge, and now he knew that he was one of the few who could find their way to the heart of the mystery of the pale wizard.

Finally, at the far end of a corridor, Zarkof held out the medallion toward a door. It opened before them. And there in the center of a large room sat a chair, glowing as if it had an inner fire.

Zarkof turned toward them with his face alight. "And there is the power. The crystal chair. Observe."

He sat in the chair, and his body suddenly glowed. Power of some sort appeared to flow into him, and he cried, "I am your servant, O Lord of Darkness."

Then the voice of another reverberated in the cavern. It seemed to come from everywhere. "Well done, wizard. I am pleased with you. Now take these two and all their people into my service."

The voice faded away, and Zarkof arose. Some of the power of the chair still glowed in his eyes. He said, "That was the voice of the Dark Lord. You have heard what he said. Are you with us or against us?"

Beorn saw his father hesitate.

"You must choose," Zarkof said. "There can be no middle ground."

And then Balog said, "We are with you, wizard. Arm us with weapons to defeat our enemies, and we will serve the Dark Lord."

For some reason, as his father gave his oath of allegiance, Beorn's heart seemed to freeze. It was as though a cold mighty fist had closed around it. He glanced fearfully at the chair, glowing still with a pale, evil light.

"Very good. Now I will go out with you. Otherwise, you would never make it alive past Shivea."

When they were outside the palace, ready to return to the village, Balog took a deep breath. "We will win over the Lowami people now. We will have a weapon that they cannot fight against. The very power of the Dark Lord."

Beorn said nothing, but he was depressed at heart. As the sleigh spun along, he kept wanting to protest. But he knew that his father was a stubborn man and that he would not go back on what he had vowed.

8

Weapons of the Yanti

One day the Sleepers were invited to join the hunt for a great whale that had gotten itself caught in the shallows of a bay. The creature could not get out, but Fairmina said, "The tide will rise, and then we will lose him. We must kill him now."

As the Sleepers climbed into small wooden-frame boats covered with waterproof hides, Wash seemed nervous. He told Josh, "I never did like boats, and that whale is big as a mountain."

The whale lay half exposed, blowing high into the air. Its top was dark blue, its belly white. Josh didn't see how anything could be done with such a monster.

The rest of the Sleepers sounded equally doubtful. Sarah and Abbey stayed on the bank with the women and rather fearfully watched them go.

"One slap of that thing's tail, and it will be all over for you," Abbey warned.

But Sarah called encouragingly, "The Lowami have done this many times."

The Lowami carefully maneuvered their small craft around the whale, which had been lying still for a time. The boats floated up beside its hulk, and the harpooners all stood.

Josh was sharing a boat with Dave. Awkwardly he got to his feet and looked at the mountain of whale in front of him. He saw Fairmina raise her harpoon and nod. As he had been instructed, he threw his weapon with all his might. He heard the others grunt as at least twenty harpooners threw their barbed spears at the same time.

Instantly the whale rose higher out of the water. He thrashed about, upsetting several of the flimsy boats.

Josh fell to the bottom of their boat, then quickly seized a paddle. Dave did the same, and they rowed out of immediate danger.

The monster stoved in two other boats, but the warriors swam away and were pulled to safety.

Then a cry of victory sounded from Fairmina's lips, and the hunters all echoed it.

"Well, I guess that means we killed our first whale." Dave wiped his face with the back of his hand and said, "Pretty messy, isn't it?"

"You know what I'm thinking?" Josh asked.

"What?"

"How do you *clean* a thing like this. I mean, I've cleaned fish that weighed ten or fifteen pounds, but look at that!"

Josh was to find out that cutting up the whale was probably the messiest job he had ever encountered.

First, all the men attached ropes to their catch and, paddling with all their might, dragged the monster to land. Then they hitched reindeer to the whale and dragged him up onto the shore.

The women descended then with long knives, the same knives used to make igloos. The blades flashed in the sun, and huge chunks of blubber began to disappear. Fires were built, and the blubber put in pots.

"What are they doing that for?" Josh asked.

"They're making oil. It's what we burn in our lamps. Also we cook our food in it," Fairmina told him.

After they'd worked for a while, Abbey was miserable. She was always very fussy about her appearance, and she cried, "I'll never get clean! Never!"

Sarah was little better off, but she managed to laugh. "It'll all wash out, and someday you'll be able to tell your grandchildren that you once helped clean a whale in Whiteland."

The cleaning of the whale went on the rest of the day.

The sun was just starting to go down when a shout attracted everyone's attention. Fairmina straightened up and said, "That's trouble!" Then she hurried forward to meet a runner, who came up gasping for breath.

"The Yanti are coming! They are coming to the village!"

Instantly Fairmina began to shout commands. The warriors all cast their cleaning tools aside and reached for their weapons.

"We've got to help," Josh said. He ordered the Sleepers to grab their bows and quivers full of arrows, which they always carried with them.

And they all began the race to head off the Yanti before they reached the village. Fairmina was, by far, the most fleet of foot. She would get so far ahead that she had to wait for the others, all the time urging them on.

They reached the valley near the village just as night was closing in. Almost at once a scout came back to say, "They're coming—right over that rise."

"Archers, take your positions! Spearmen, get ready for battle! Fight for your homes, your wives, and your children!"

And the battle line was drawn.

Out of breath, Josh gasped to Sarah, "It looks like we got here just in time."

"They're headed straight for the village all right."

"Well, we can stop them. We whipped them the last time."

The Lowami warriors all waited, scarcely breathing. Arrows were notched on bowstrings, and spears were clutched firmly.

And then a cry of terror sounded, for over the rise came not Yantis but three ice wraiths.

Cold fear closed around Josh's own heart. This was no Yanti raid. They could stand before that. But three ice wraiths . . .

"And see—they have *riders!*" Denhelm cried.

Even in the growing darkness it was obvious that the ice wraiths had been fitted with harness, and on the back of each sat a warrior, holding a sword high in the air and urging the monsters on. Behind them came a line of Yanti warriors, totally protected by the fierce ice wraiths.

"How can this be?" Denhelm gasped. "No man can tame an ice wraith."

It was at that moment that Fairmina showed her true courage. Other hearts may have quailed, but she cried out, "Do not be afraid! We are warriors of the Lowami! Aim for the riders on their backs! They somehow control the wraiths!"

"If nobody can tame an ice wraith," Josh muttered, "this has something to do with the Dark Lord. I know it has. He can control things like that."

There was no time for more talk. The wraiths were advancing swiftly toward the Lowami battle line.

"Shoot!" Fairmina cried, and the air was filled with hissing, whistling arrows. Most bounced harmlessly off the wraiths' tough hides. "The riders!" Fairmina ordered. "Shoot the *riders!*"

The ice wraiths came on, and those who stood against them fell. With sinking heart, Josh saw warrior after warrior go down under their slashing claws and saberlike teeth. He could not help admiring the men's courage, but at the same time he knew it was foolish. "Come, Sarah—Dave!" he urged. "We've got to get close enough to hit those riders."

Sarah and Dave grunted, and each notched an arrow.

Fairmina was involved in a raging fight alongside her father. The line of Yanti warriors was now in the battle, and swords were clashing.

"You take the rider on the left, Dave!" Josh cried. "You take the one on the right, Sarah! I'll get the middle one."

The three separated, and Josh advanced until the dark form of the center ice wraith loomed over him. Now he could see the face of the warrior on its back. He was grinning and shouting for the monster to kill.

Josh didn't want to slay the rider, but he had seen too many friends, companions that he had learned to trust, going down under the wraiths' fangs and claws. He bent his bow, drew a dead bead, and released the arrow. It caught the warrior above the armor that protected his chest. He fell backwards.

Instantly the rider's ice wraith stopped its advance. It seemed paralyzed.

Josh glanced to the right and saw that Sarah was in trouble.

He raced over to help, and the two of them managed to take the second rider out of the saddle. His wraith too then stood dead still.

Josh quickly turned to see that Dave had finally knocked the third wraith rider out of the harness.

"They don't know what to do when their riders are gone!" Dave yelled.

"I see that!" Josh shouted back. "Let's go help the others!"

He heard the Yanti commander order, "Back! Mount the ice wraiths! They must be controlled!"

But then another factor entered. Volka advanced into the fray, swinging his club like a terrible scythe. Yantis fell right and left before him until most of the Yanti force began a disorganized retreat.

At this point, Fairmina apparently lost her head. Josh saw her run straight toward the uneven battle line. Almost at once she was engaged in a deadly duel with a skillful warrior, one who appeared to match her in ability and strength.

And then reinforcements arrived to cover the Yanti retreat. The fresh troops drove Chief Denhelm and his forces backward, and the ranks closed.

"They've captured Fairmina!" Josh yelled. "We've got to get her back!"

But there was no hope of this. Although the Yanti forces were in retreat, there was no breaking through their line.

Denhelm, who had taken a wound in the arm, stood holding it. "My daughter," he moaned. "Fairmina!"

Fairmina stood surrounded by a ring of Yanti warriors that included Chief Balog and his son. She had soon learned that it was the son she had dueled with. Neither had won the duel, for she had been overpowered by other warriors and her sword taken from her. She would have been slain, but the son—Beorn—had leaped to her side, saying, "No! She is a courageous woman, a warrior. Foolish, but brave."

Fairmina stood straight. She had been wounded slightly on the neck and the back of her hand, but she paid no heed. "You are no men!" she spat. "Beasts must fight for you!"

The Yanti chief was understandably angry over the way the battle had gone. "Take her back, and she will be a hostage. Maybe we will offer her as sacrifice to the Dark Lord."

The chief's son stood watching as warriors bound her hands. He stepped close enough to say, "You have courage."

"Do not speak to me, Yanti! You are cowards—all of you—to fight under the spell of the Dark Lord!"

A rope was placed around Fairmina's neck, and the Yanti guard pulled her roughly.

But the chief's son spoke sharply to him. "She does not need that!" Drawing his knife, he slashed the rope away. "You will be well treated," he said.

Fairmina stared at him and raised her chin. "I will not be well treated! It is not in you or your people to be generous!"

The chief's son said nothing more. He turned away, and the Yanti began the long march back to their village.

9

What to Do About Fairmina

It was a pitiful group of survivors who made their way back to the Lowami village. Almost half of their number had severe wounds. Volka pulled four of their dead on a quickly thrown together sled. By the time they arrived, all were totally exhausted except, of course, Volka, who never seemed to tire.

Mat looked up at the giant and grumbled, "I wish one time you'd get tired, Volka."

"Volka never get tired," the giant replied. He looked back toward the bodies of the slain on the sled he was pulling. "Too bad. Nice men."

Tam tried to look on the bright side as usual. "It could have been worse. If those ice wraiths hadn't been stopped, we'd *all* be dead. But here we are, mostly with just a few scratches."

Mat held out his arm. His sleeve was ripped from elbow to wrist. "Look at that." He pulled it back to reveal a deep wound.

"Come on, then," Tam said hurriedly. "We'd better get you sewed up. I'll do the job myself to make sure it's done right."

"I wouldn't trust you to sew up my underwear!" Mat complained. Nevertheless, he was weak from loss of blood and soon was lying on a table while Tam cared for the wound.

"There," Tam said. "You'll be good as new."

"No, I won't! I'll have a scar as long as I live!" Mat

tried to sit up but fell back dizzily. "Room's going around," he muttered.

"Lie there, brother," Tam said. "I'll get you some hot soup. Then you can sleep."

The entire Long House was filled with the wounded. Josh watched the women, led by the chief's wife, move quickly among them. Rimah was known as an expert with herbs, and she had brewed a strong mixture that brought relief to the pain of the wounded.

She stopped beside Wash, who had a gash across his right calf. "Drink this," Rimah said. "You will soon feel better."

Wash looked up with fatigue on his face. "Thank you, ma'am." He took the cup of hot liquid and sipped it. "What is this?" he said.

"Something to take the pain away and make you sleep."

"I don't know if I want to sleep," he muttered. "I'll dream about those ice wraiths."

But then he looked around at the long faces of the other Sleepers as they bound up each other's wounds, and he said, "Hey, it was pretty bad, but we've had worse."

"Worse! I don't know when," Dave said. He was bandaging Jake's neck, which had been scraped by a Yanti ax. Peering at the wound closely, he said, "A little bit deeper, and that would have got you."

"Well, a miss is good as a mile." Jake tried to smile, but obviously he was still shaken over the experience. "It didn't bother me," he said slowly, "thinking about facing the Yanti. But when those ice wraiths came over that hill, I'm telling you it did something to me."

Denhelm came by. His face was grave. "It was very

brave of you to charge in and shoot the riders from the ice wraiths. You saved the day with your courage."

Josh knew that the chief was grieved to the heart over the loss of his daughter. He said quietly, "Sir, we've got to get Fairmina back. As soon as we can pull ourselves together, we'll take her away from the Yanti."

"Balog is no fool. By this time they will have figured out that the ice wraiths are no stronger than their riders. The next time we meet them, you can believe that the riders will be well armored. Balog is the son of one of the most noted warriors in history. The son is more impetuous and not as wise, but he has Magon for a counselor. No, we needn't look for any mercy from them in the future. As a matter of fact, I wouldn't be surprised but that they return very soon."

"How did they ever manage to get the ice wraiths tamed?" Jake murmured. "I thought they were untamable beasts."

"I fear that it is the power of the Dark Lord at work. I have heard that he has power over animals, and he has granted some of his power to Zarkof."

"Zarkof, the pale wizard," Josh said thoughtfully.

"He is an evil man, and I fear that Balog and his people have fallen under his influence. A sad, grievous day for us." Pain swept across his face, and his shoulders sagged. "We must give my daughter up for lost."

"Do you think they'll kill her?" Sarah whispered, her eyes large with fright.

"They are capable of it. Especially with Zarkof counseling them. I've heard he believes in human sacrifice. I don't know that to be true," he added hurriedly, "but in any case, they will never let Fairmina go. I expect them to use her as a hostage."

At this, Chief Denhelm walked away.

"I feel so sorry for him," Abbey said. "His only daughter in the hands of those awful people. I wish they were all dead."

"Don't say that," Sarah said quickly. "I'm sure they're not all evil."

"They're allied with the Dark Lord, aren't they?"

"They're blinded, and they need to be enlightened," Sarah said. "We've seen it happen before. The Dark Lord has powers, but Goél can brush the shadows away from their minds. And Goél will help us know what to do."

For the next few days, Denhelm kept a guard surrounding the camp. Everyone knew he expected a raid from the Yanti at any moment, and everyone knew that there was no defense from tamed ice wraiths. The whole camp was on alert, ready to flee at the first warning of the outpost guards.

On the third night, Denhelm called a meeting of the council. There were empty places at the table, which must have saddened him. Rimah came and stood behind him, her hands on his shoulders as he outlined the situation.

"We all know," he said, "that we are in grave danger. We owe our lives now to three of the Sleepers. I apologize to them for having ever doubted their ability." He smiled faintly through the pain that was in his heart. "I took them a little lightly, but Goél always knows how to send just the right aid."

"I wish Goél himself would come," Josh broke in. He had intended to say nothing, but the wish was heavy on his heart. "Cannot we send for him, Chief?"

"And where would you go to find him?"

Josh realized that there was truth in this. Goél did

not have a street address where one could go and knock on the door and find him at home. He was everywhere—and he was nowhere. Despair came over Josh then. "But we've got to do something about Fairmina."

Talk ran around the table for some time, until finally Rimah spoke up. She had a gentle voice, but all the men immediately listened. Josh could tell that they had great respect for the wife of the chief.

"I am not one who has a great many dreams," she said quietly. "I would leave that to the ancient ones and the priests who are among us. But for three nights in a row, I've had the same dream, and it comes to me that I should share it with you."

"What sort of a dream was it, wife?" Denhelm asked quietly, his eyes fixed on her with alert interest.

"I hardly know how to describe it. It comes quickly and flashes before my mind, and then it is gone. It has to do with the Yanti. And I have seen Fairmina in the dream three times."

"Is she safe?" Denhelm cried and then waited as if to receive a blow.

"In the dream I see her closely guarded but no harm has come to her. She seems not to be wounded, and she has kept her courage."

"What else is in the dream?"

"There is a man. I have never seen him before, but I know that he is evil. He wears a black cloak with a hood, and around his neck there is a gold medallion. It has an emblem on it that I could not clearly see. All I know is that he is speaking constantly to Balog and the Yanti council. He seems to be enclosed with a cloud so that I could not see his face clearly."

"That sounds like Zarkof," one of the older council members said. "I have seen him twice. He always wears that black cloak with a hood over his face, and he wears a gold emblem with a crooked lightning bolt on it—the sign of the Dark Lord."

"Was there more to the dream?"

"I see—I see the Sleepers going through a passage to a dark cavern. A horrible creature is waiting. I can never see what it is, but I know it is most terrible."

"Is that all?" Denhelm asked.

"Except for one thing more. Each time, Fairmina looks up and motions to me, and I hear her saying, 'Come.'"

"Then the dream is clear," Josh said. "We must go and rescue her."

"But who must go?" Denhelm demanded.

"All of us!" Josh said.

"We cannot leave our women and children here unguarded," Denhelm said quietly.

"Oh, I didn't think about that."

"And where would you go?" Denhelm asked.

"Why, to the Yanti camp."

"And do you think they would open the door so that you could walk right in?" a man jeered. "They will have guards out, even as we do."

"But we have to do something," Sarah said. "We can't leave Fairmina there."

"Yes, we must do something," the chief said. "I wish Goél were here, for I have no wisdom. If they have the ice wraiths mounted and under control, we are doomed sooner or later."

"Why can't we sneak up on 'em and surprise 'em?" Reb asked. His eyes glowed with excitement. "If we catch 'em off guard before they can mount those ice wraiths, we'll have a chance."

"Their tribe is larger than ours," Denhelm said.

"And as for sneaking up on them, they have many good hunters. They are more apt to sneak up on *us*, I think, with their greater numbers."

Silence fell over the room, and the chief bowed his head. He seemed to be thinking hard, and again Rimah put her hands on his shoulders. Reaching up, he held them under his own. Then he looked up with grief in his eyes. "We must wait until someone has word from Goél. Otherwise, we may throw our lives away."

It seemed to Josh that waiting could lead to nothing but disaster. "If the ice wraiths come before we hear from Goél, we'll all be lost," he whispered to Reb.

"I think you're right, but it's Denhelm's decision. He's responsible for the whole tribe."

"If it were me," Jake whispered, "I'd go for it. I don't want to go down with my bat on my shoulder. We could go down trying, anyway."

But the will of Denhelm prevailed, and they waited.

Josh thought of the ice wraiths out there in the darkness somewhere. They might come at any time, and this knowledge did not make for good sleeping.

10

Captive and Captor

Outwardly, Fairmina endured her captivity with courage and strength. Three days passed, and so far she had said not a word to her captors. Balog brought her before the council twice, but when they questioned her about her people and her father, she did not open her lips a single time. This had infuriated him, and he had said, "Let her have nothing to eat until she decides to talk!"

During the next twenty-four hours Fairmina was given all the water she wanted but no food.

She was kept in a stone house approximately ten feet square. There was no fire, but there was a cot with furs on it for covering. The only other furniture was a small table and a chair. She spent hours walking back and forth like a caged animal, aware that the guards were watching her through the grates built on each side of her small prison.

Once a day they took her out for exercise but kept a heavy rope tied around her neck. The end was held by one of her two guards. The other guard, Deur, kept an arrow notched in his bow, and she knew that at the least provocation he would be glad to send it through her.

This was the only time that she had any chance at all to escape. Her mind worked constantly. She thought of how she might jerk the guard off stride with the rope he held, then run to him and draw his sword and finish him off. But there was always the other guard, a small, swarthy man with alert gray eyes. He watched her continually and from time to time would move his arrow back and forth as if yearning to send it into her heart.

"If I could just get rid of him for three minutes, I could overcome the other one. Then no one would catch me."

But the Yanti had chosen their guards well. The small archer never took his eyes off her.

On the second day without food, she was taken out for exercise and the noose tightened around her neck. This was an indignity to Fairmina, but she endured it for the sake of getting outside the four prison walls.

When she stepped out today, she saw that the skies were clear. The sun was warming the earth. Tiny rivulets of melting snow had formed along the path through the trees. She walked toward the river, much aware of the presence of Deur. She had heard that he was the best archer of all the Yantis. She also knew that no matter how fast she was, an arrow was swifter.

Still, there was always a chance. She was sure that sooner or later someone would come for her. Still, an attempted rescue would be hopeless, for Balog had thrown out a triple ring of guards, expecting just such a move.

"Good morning."

Fairmina turned with surprise to see Beorn, the son of Chief Balog. He had come up quietly. She was irritated with herself for not hearing him. She did not answer.

"Do you mind if I join you on your walk?"

Fairmina looked closely at the chief's son. She had to admit he was a fair man indeed. Tall and strong with dark hair and eyes. "Do as you please," she heard herself saying. "I'm your prisoner. I could not prevent you."

Beorn suddenly reached over and took the leather thong from the guard. "Take a break, Gaylon," he said. "I'll guard the prisoner. You go, too, Deur."

"No. I am commanded by your father to always watch the prisoner."

Fairmina suspected that Deur was a fanatical warrior who would never disobey a direct order from the chief.

Beorn shrugged. "Very well, but I don't see any need for a noose around our captive's neck. She can't outrun an arrow."

"It was your father's order."

"Well, I can't countermand my father's orders." Beorn turned to Fairmina. "Come. I know you need exercise."

"I do. I get cramped." It was more than she had intended to say, and she immediately regretted the words.

"I know how that is. Would you like to run a little bit?"

"Yes!" she exclaimed.

Beorn grinned and then winked at her. "Very well. We will run." Glancing back at the archer, he said, "Follow us, Deur. Don't get too far behind."

"I will not be out of arrow range! You can believe that."

"Come along, Princess."

"You call me that? I am your captive."

"But you are the daughter of Chief Denhelm. That makes you a princess."

Fairmina did not reply but began running lightly along the path. The noose was still about her neck, but the chief's son held it loosely. He kept pace with her and had a smooth, swift, even gait. Glancing back over her shoulder, she saw that Deur, who was short and stubby-legged, was having a difficult time. And a thought came to her. *If we get far enough ahead, I could snatch the dagger out of this one's sheath, cut his throat, and then dart into the trees. That lumbering archer could never catch me. If he missed his first arrow, I would be free.*

"I wouldn't even think of it if I were you."

She startled. "Think of what?"

"Snatching my dagger, killing me, and then making a run for it."

He grinned, looking very handsome with his teeth white against his dark skin. "Because it's what I would have thought of if I were you. It would be the best chance you would have for escape."

Fairmina was chagrined at having her plan laid bare so quickly. She did not answer but kept up an even stride. Then she said, "The archer may get impatient if we get too far ahead. He may shoot me anyway and say I was trying to escape."

"Then let's go the other way."

The two whirled and jogged back toward the archer.

Deur scowled and said, "Stop that running!"

"You don't give orders to the son of the chief, Deur. You just attend to your business."

They sailed by the infuriated archer, and he lumbered after them. Fairmina knew it would be hard for him to keep an arrow notched on the string.

"A little excitement is a good thing. For over two weeks I was once the prisoner of a tribe we were at war with."

"My people?"

"No. Another tribe, farther north. A long time ago. I nearly went crazy locked up in a cell about like the one you're in."

It was an interesting side of Beorn's character, and Fairmina found herself interested in the young man. "You probably won't tell me, but how did you ever get the ice wraiths to let you harness them and accept riders?"

"I would tell you if I could, but I cannot. I do not understand it myself."

"It has something to do with Zarkof, I venture."

He gave her a surprised look. "I'm sure it has something to do with Zarkof," he said. "When he brought us the ice wraiths, they were already harnessed. He'd put some kind of spell on them. Either he or the Dark Lord. In any case, the scheme didn't work too well, did it?"

"No. Three of the Seven Sleepers charged in and shot the riders."

"I saw it. They were very brave. Who are the 'Seven Sleepers'?"

"They are the servants of Goél."

"My grandfather believes in Goél."

This caught Fairmina totally by surprise. "He does!" she exclaimed. "I can't believe it!"

"How can you not believe it?"

"Because Goél is kind and is for peace."

"So is my grandfather Magon. He was a famous warrior in his time. Now he is old, but he still talks about Goél. He met him twice when he was a young man. He told me recently that he wished he had kept up the acquaintance. That he feels the Yanti would have been stronger if they would have gone the way of Goél."

"The Dark Lord and Goél are engaged in a struggle

for the world. I understand that much. That makes us enemies."

Beorn jogged silently by her side for a time. Then he said, "I wish we were not enemies. I wish this stupid war had never happened. I've hated it ever since I first knew about it as a child."

"Why, so have I!" Fairmina exclaimed.

Then Deur shouted, "Slower, or I'll put an arrow in her!" and she slowed her pace. Glancing back, she saw that indeed Deur had his bow drawn. "I suppose he would do it."

"He probably would," Beorn said. "Here. Let me get behind you. He wouldn't put an arrow through me."

"Aren't you afraid that I will get away?"

"I wish you were away," he said. "You have no business here."

"What do they plan to do with me?"

He hesitated.

Perhaps he did not wish to tell her the truth. Perhaps some had already suggested executing her. Perhaps she would be given as a slave to the Dark Lord.

She heard him clear his throat. "I do not want to see anything happen to you, Princess. I do not make war on women."

"I am a warrior of the Lowami," she said over her shoulder. "I take my chances in war like any of the men."

But the chief's son said, "I know you are an excellent warrior, and I understand that you have learned the art of war from your father. Nevertheless, to fight against women goes against all I believe in."

Somehow this saying both disturbed and pleased Fairmina. She had spent much of her life trying to earn her place in a world ruled by men. She thought she had worked harder at being a good warrior than anyone else, and she valued her place at her father's side when the battle trumpets sounded. Still, as the tall young man behind her spoke so gently, his words gave her a warm feeling.

"You have a gentle spirit. I am surprised."

"What did you expect? That all Yantis are wild beasts?"

Suddenly Fairmina laughed. "Of course. I always thought of you as wild beasts. Isn't that the way you think of the Lowami?"

"I'm afraid so. I listened to some of the tales of the older warriors, and they make you sound vicious indeed."

"I think we both have listened to those old tales a great deal. Too much, perhaps."

Now the two began walking, side by side, slowly, with the scowling Deur just behind them. "He would like to put an arrow in me," she said.

"He hates all Lowami. As a matter of fact, I think he hates most everybody. He's loyal only to my father. He's a good archer, though, so I do warn you, Princess —don't ever try to outrun one of his shafts. He can pin a fly to a tree from a hundred paces."

"I would like to shoot against him sometime."

"I'm sure my father wouldn't permit that. Think what it would mean if a woman beat his best archer."

"It would give him a little humility, perhaps. I'm sure he needs it."

"I think, perhaps, he does. But then, don't we all? I think I see a little pride in you, Princess."

"Pride is not a bad thing. It is good."

"That depends," Beorn said. "It can eat away at a man—or a woman—and destroy them. Humility is better, or so my grandfather says."

They walked on, talking. Suddenly Beorn said, "You didn't eat yesterday."

"No. Your father forbade it."

"Well, he gave no command for today. So before he has a chance to do so, come along."

"I will not eat."

"Surely you will not refuse to join me. That would be discourteous."

Actually Fairmina was starving. Besides, the cold weather drained the energy out of a person quickly, and she knew that she had to keep up her strength if she was going to survive.

"We'll go to my home. My mother always has something bubbling over the fire."

"I don't want to meet your father."

"He won't be there. He's gone on a hunt. Just my mother. Come along, Deur. We're going to my house."

"Your father said nothing about that."

"Take it up with him when he comes back. Let's go, Princess. I'm hungry myself."

Fairmina walked alongside him. The rope hung loosely around her neck, and he held the other end loosely in his hand. It was only a formality, she knew. He had shown great courtesy.

"This is our house. Come inside," Beorn said. "Deur, wait here at the door."

"I am not to let her out of my sight."

"Don't be a fool, Deur! There's only one door. She's visiting my *mother.*"

The archer scowled, but he did not argue further.

As soon as she entered the chief's house, Beorn said, "Mother, you know this is Princess Fairmina. This is my mother, Olah."

"I am glad to see you, my daughter," Olah said

kindly. "I remember our people well. I was only fourteen when I was captured, but I knew your father and your mother. They were very good to me."

Fairmina was almost speechless before the quiet grace of this woman. She bowed slightly, saying, "My mother has spoken of you often."

"We were friends. We were the same age, you know. I would give anything to see her again."

"Perhaps that may come," Fairmina said.

A shadow crossed the eyes of the woman, and she said, "I pray that it will be so."

"Mother, she hasn't had anything to eat. Can you prepare us something?"

"Of course. You two sit and talk. I have some fresh stew, and I baked bread. Sit down."

When the food was put before Fairmina, the other two joined her at the table. She had to restrain herself from gulping down the stew. But she forced herself to eat slowly. "This is very good!" she exclaimed.

"My mother's the best cook in the world." Beorn took his mother's hand and kissed it. It was a gesture that caught Fairmina's eye. She remembered that her own mother had once said, "Watch how a man treats his mother before you marry him. He will treat you the same way." The act pleased her.

That meal changed Princess Fairmina's mind about the Yanti tribe. *If these two are gentle, as I see they are, then there must be others as well.*

After Beorn had eaten, he said, "I will leave the princess with you, if you don't mind, Mother. I have some work to do, but this house will be much better for her than that little hut."

"Of course!"

"Father may not like it."

107

"I will explain it to him."

Beorn grinned and winked at Fairmina. "That means she'll tell him how to think. She does that with father and me both. I'll be back later."

It was a pleasant day for Fairmina. She helped her hostess sew clothing out of soft reindeer skin. She helped her prepare some food. All in all, she felt a peace that she had not felt since she had been captured.

Outside, Beorn went about his work, but during the course of the day he heard a man repeating a tale to another. It seemed he had once been enslaved by Zarkof but had escaped.

"Nobody will ever get in. There's a monster guarding it. A big spiderlike thing."

His companion was listening with avid curiosity. "What's he guarding in there?"

Beorn leaned forward to catch the answer.

"He's got a magic chair down under the castle. I don't understand it, but I heard two of his lieutenants talking. He gets all his power from that chair, and it's guarded by that big spider."

Just as I suspected. Power lies in that crystal chair, Beorn thought. He had thought of little else since making that visit with his father to the white fortress. He remembered the glowing chair and how it had put its glow into the wizard's body.

Later in the day, he returned home and found his mother and the princess laughing together.

The princess stood as soon as he came in. "I suppose it's time for me to go back to my cell."

"I think it might be better if you were there when my father returns," he said with some embarrassment.

"I'll have you here for another visit." Olah smiled. Then she kissed the girl. "Don't worry, my dear. It will turn out well."

He and the princess walked back toward Fairmina's prison as Deur walked behind, still scowling and fingering his arrow.

Fairmina said, "Your mother's a very lovely woman."

"The loveliest I've ever known."

"What a nice thing to say!"

"It's true enough."

As they waited for the guard to open her cell, Fairmina turned and smiled. She whispered, "Thank you for a lovely day. It was very kind of you."

"I wish I could do more."

She hesitated, then leaned forward and spoke so quietly that the guards could not hear. "Beware of the Dark Lord. I know about him, Beorn. He will be a hard master. You are in danger of being enslaved as much as I am right now."

She went inside then, and the guard slammed the door and fastened the padlock.

Beorn turned away, but he couldn't forget the girl's words. *You are in danger of being enslaved.* It was a thought that sent fear through him, for he loved his freedom. He went to see his grandfather.

Magon listened quietly as Beorn spoke of the princess. "She is a beautiful young woman and very brave," his grandfather said finally. "I wish she were back with her people."

Beorn glanced quickly at his grandfather. "Maybe we could persuade father to let her go."

"I think not. He's a stubborn man, and he will never admit he's wrong."

Beorn sat quietly, looking glumly at the floor. "This war's a bad thing."

"It always has been. War is never pleasant."

11

A Rebellious Son

*Z*arkof, as always, had his fears as he entered the underground caverns. He knew that the medallion he had been given by the Dark Lord had always stopped the monster spider in her tracks. Still, Shivea was a frightening creature, and a cold sweat broke out on the wizard's brow. He wiped it away, muttering, "What if sometime the spell doesn't work?" A shiver went over him, and he thought of those poison-dripping fangs. It was more than he cared to think of, and he hurried on.

Shivea suddenly appeared to his left, her many faceted eyes glowing like tiny red furnaces. Her fangs were bared, and at once Zarkof held up the medallion. For one terrifying moment it seemed to him that the spell was not going to work—but then the creature slithered backward, her claws making a scraping noise across the stone floor.

I don't think it's worth it having her for a guard. She's going to get loose and kill me one of these days. I think I'll put her out of the way.

Zarkof had had this thought before. Still, he needed her. He was determined that nothing would get to the crystal chair. It had been given to him by the Dark Lord himself, and it was only when he sat in it that the power seemed to flow. Zarkof was an old man now, older than anyone he knew. He had come into this cavern for scores of years, and in some way the power of the chair kept his true age from showing.

Now he entered the room where the chair sat in the midst, giving off its luminous green glow.

Eagerly, as always, Zarkof threw himself into the chair. He was like a drug addict who lived for this particular moment. At once he felt the power of the Dark Lord reaching out from his own stronghold far to the south.

What have you to report?

The voice spoke inside Zarkof's head, but he answered aloud. "Things are going well, sire."

Have you obliterated the Lowami tribe?

"Well, not exactly, my lord—"

Not exactly! And what does that mean? They are either exterminated, or they are not. Answer me.

Stammering wildly, Zarkof explained that the warriors had been shot out of their harnesses.

Who shot them out?

"I understand—although I was not there myself— that it was three of the young people they call Sleepers."

Instantly a tremendous pain shot through Zarkof's brain. It flowed down through his entire body, and he would have fallen from the chair except for an unseen power's keeping him there.

Finally the pain ebbed away, leaving him feeble and helpless.

The Seven Sleepers. You must kill them! Do you understand me? They are more dangerous than all the Lowami tribe or anyone else. If you fail me in this, you will die.

"I will not fail. I promise you, my lord. They will die."

And kill the girl, Fairmina. Send her head to the Lowami. To Denhelm, her father.

"Yes, my lord. At once."

The glow faded, and it took all the strength Zarkof had to get up from the chair. It was not the first time the Dark Lord had brought this pain to him. It was something he dreaded and did everything he could to avoid.

Fingering the medallion, he staggered out of the secret room, saying, "Kill the princess—kill the princess—kill the Sleepers!"

"I must do it," he said, "or he will have my life. I know he will!" He saw Shivea's red eyes glowing in the darkness. He showed the medallion and scurried past.

He said to the first guard he encountered, "Get me a messenger."

"Yes, sire."

When the messenger came, Zarkof said, "I will not write this down. It must be vocal."

"Yes, sire."

"Tell Chief Balog that I command him to kill Princess Fairmina."

"Yes, sire. At once."

"Repeat the message."

"Chief Balog is to kill the Princess Fairmina."

"Go quickly."

The wizard fled to the top of his fortress, where he was attended by blank-eyed slaves. He began drinking himself into insensibility, but he was already rehearsing his next speech to the Dark Lord. "The Princess Fairmina has been killed, and the Seven Sleepers are dead as well . . ."

Beorn had been highly confused ever since the day he took the princess to visit his mother. He constantly heard talk of executing her and could hardly bear to think of it. He had protested, "She is but a woman!"

"She is the heir of Denhelm. She is his war chief. Woman though she be," Balog, his father, exclaimed, "she cannot live!"

Beorn talked with his mother and with his grandfather many times. The three of them all opposed taking the life of the princess.

"It will bring evil on our tribe. There is no honor in it," Magon said grimly. "We must not permit my son to do this."

Olah shook her head. "He is stubborn. How can we prevent it?"

"We must do something," Beorn said.

After this conversation, he went to visit the princess. As usual, he brought her out of her prison house, although the noose was around her neck and he held the end. He wanted to get far enough away to talk freely. They had done this now for several days and had gotten to know each other quite well.

"Something is bothering you, is it not, Beorn?" the princess inquired.

"Why do you ask that?"

"Your face is not hard to read. I can see trouble in your eyes."

"Can you? I never was much at hiding things."

"Your mother has eyes like that. You know exactly what she's thinking."

"Yes, you do. And they're always good thoughts."

As they strolled along, a dog came up and sniffed at Beorn's hand. He patted its shaggy head and said, "Be off with you now." He turned to Fairmina. "Are you being well cared for?"

"Very well."

114

"It's very uncomfortable in that prison. I'll see what I can do to make it more comfortable."

Fairmina appeared puzzled, as though she knew something was on his mind. "I wish you'd tell me what's troubling you—not that I could do anything about it. After all, you're the captor, and I'm the captive."

"To be truthful, I'm worried about you."

"Is that all you have to think about? An enemy."

"I do not think of you, Princess, as my enemy."

Fairmina stared at him. "You don't?"

"Of course not. You don't think of me as an enemy, I hope."

"I did when I was captured. But—" She hesitated and then added, "You've been very kind to me, Beorn. You and your mother have changed my whole idea about what the Yanti are like. If two of you are that kind, there must be many others."

"We are like other people, I suppose. Some of us are kind, some not so kind."

"It's certainly that way with my people," the princess said. "Maybe with all peoples."

After they had walked for some time, Beorn made up his mind. "I will talk to my father. I will ask him to release you."

"He will never do that."

"He may. My grandfather has great influence with him. Freeing you would make Grandfather happy. And my mother as well. At least I will try."

Impulsively the princess put out her hand. It was at once enclosed by Beorn's. He squeezed it hard, and she said, "Thank you for your kindness."

"I make no promises, but I will do what I can."

Beorn went at once to his father and without preamble said, "Father, I want to ask a favor."

115

"What is it, Beorn?"

"I think we should release Princess Fairmina."

"Have you lost your mind!"

"I've been thinking about this whole business of war. If she's a sample of what the Lowami are like, we're fools to fight them."

"What do you know about it? You're a boy!"

"I think I know honesty and courage and truth when I see it."

"She's the *enemy!*"

"We've made her that way. This war takes the brains out of people. We don't have any sense left. We just fight and fight"—Beorn's voice rose—"and men and women die, and nothing is ever settled!"

"Don't talk to me that way, boy!"

"It's true, isn't it?" He was angry now. "It was the same way when you were young! It was the same way when Grandfather was a boy! The stupid war goes on, it never gets settled, and people die! And all for what?"

"You cannot know about these things!"

Just then a voice speaking outside the door interrupted their argument. "I must see the chief. I have a message from the wizard."

"Wait here," Beorn heard the guard on duty say. "I'll see if he'll have you."

The guard stepped inside. "Sire, I'm sorry to interrupt, but there's a messenger here from Zarkof."

"Send him in." Then Balog turned to his son. His face was still red with anger. "I'll hear no more of this!"

Beorn turned to go out, but then he stopped and looked at the messenger from Zarkof. He was a muscular, swarthy man with an evil look.

The man said, "I have a message, Chief Balog."

"Well, what's the message? Give it to me."

"It's not written down, sire." He glanced at Beorn. "It's for your ears alone."

"This is my son. He can hear."

"Very well. Zarkof says you are to kill Princess Fairmina."

A chill ran through Beorn, and he turned to his father. Shock appeared to run through the chief too. *Surely he won't do it*, Beorn thought.

But Balog, it seemed, had fallen more under the power of the pale wizard than his son had realized. He was trembling, but he nodded. "It shall be done."

As soon as the messenger left, Beorn cried, "Father, you can't do it!"

"I must do it. We can only win with the help of Zarkof and the ice wraiths. I must do it. After all, she's a warrior. She took her chances."

For one long moment, Beorn stared at his father's face. He had always loved and respected his father, but something had happened to Balog since the contact with Zarkof. *He's not the same man. He's not himself,* Beorn thought. He left without another word. Even as he went out, he knew what he had to do.

Beorn went to the prison and said to Deur, "Bring out the princess."

"You've already walked with her today!" the archer snapped.

"You hear me, Deur? Do what I say!"

As the other guard watched, Deur finally nodded grudgingly.

The princess looked at Beorn in surprise. It was the first time he had come twice in the same day. "What is it?"

"Come. We must talk."

The guard placed the rope around her neck as she

stepped outside and, as usual, handed the other end to Beorn.

"You can wait here," Beorn told him, "or take a break. I'll be responsible."

"Yes, sire."

It was useless, of course, to talk to Deur.

To Fairmina, Beorn murmured, "We'll walk down to the river."

They walked the path that they always took, and Beorn was silent. When they got far enough ahead of Deur, he said quietly, "You must leave this place at once."

Fairmina gave him a startled look. "How can I do that?"

"You must trust me. I will make a way. I will take care of Deur, but you must go at once."

Fairmina continued to stare at him. "What has happened?"

Struggling with the truth, Beorn finally said, "My father is not himself. He is under the power of the pale wizard." He hesitated, then said, "A message has just come from Zarkof—an order to execute you at once. Even now my father is probably giving the orders. You are a fleet runner. Let me tell you what to do. When you leave here, follow the river for three miles, then cross over it at . . ." He gave her instructions. "The warriors will be after you with dogs, but if you use the edge of the river from time to time, that will wipe out your scent. Follow what I've said, and you'll have a chance."

"But what about you?"

"There's no time, Fairmina." His voice lowered, and he said, "You are a lovely girl outside and inside even more lovely."

Fairmina seemed unable to say a word.

Then he said, "We're almost at the river. When I tell you, jerk the rope off your neck and run like the wind."

"What about Deur?"

"I will take care of Deur."

They were at the river now, and he said, "There's the river path."

"Yes, but I can't let you do this, Beorn."

"You have no choice. Are you ready?"

"Yes," she said, and her eyes were warm. "I will never forget this, nor will my people."

"May Goél be with you. Run fleet as the deer, and may you be safe."

Suddenly Beorn stopped, turned around, and called, "Deur, come here."

The archer's face grew suspicious. "What is it?"

Beorn did not answer. He let the small archer get within five paces and then, still holding the end of Fairmina's rope, asked, "Is that a good arrow you have? Does it fly true?"

Deur looked down at his arrow with puzzlement. "Why, of course . . ."

He never got to say another word, for suddenly strong hands seized him. His bow was ripped from his hands, and he found himself pinioned face down, unable to move.

"Run, Princess! Run!"

Deur struggled frantically, but Beorn was strong.

He watched until Fairmina disappeared, then got to his feet. "Come, Deur. You must tell my father what happened."

"Have you lost your mind, Beorn? He'll have you killed in her place!"

"We will see what kind of a man I have for a father. Just come. Pick up your arrows and your bow."

Thirty minutes later the council was hurriedly called together. Beorn's mother was present. Magon was there. Balog was shouting and screaming. "Do you know what he's done, this traitor son of mine? He's let her go!"

"Good. The best day's work he ever did," Magon said, his face alive with pleasure.

"Father, be quiet! You are not the chief any longer. I am!"

"Be careful how you speak to your father, Balog," Olah said softly. "You know what is said about showing respect to the elders, especially to a chief."

"He is not the chief! I am the chief, and my orders have been disobeyed!"

Beorn said nothing. When first challenged, he'd simply said, "It was wrong to keep her here, and it would be a terrible crime to have obeyed the orders of Zarkof to kill her."

"If you were anyone except my son, I would have your head taken from your shoulders!"

"I knew that might be my fate," Beorn said calmly.

Balog pulled at his hair. "Leave this place! Take what you can carry, and I never want to look upon your face again! Out with him!"

Two warriors roughly seized Beorn, and ten minutes later he started off with what he could carry.

His mother and his grandfather were waiting at the edge of the village. Each took one of his hands and held him.

"Do not be discouraged, my boy," Magon said. "Things are dark now, but these things have a way of working out."

"And do not hate your father."

"I don't, Mother. I know he's under the spell of the evil wizard."

"Exactly," Magon said, "and some day we will find a way to get him back."

"Never give up, Beorn," Olah said. Tears rose to her eyes. "May you be safe wherever you go, and may you be back soon."

"Good-bye, Mother. Good-bye, Grandfather."

As Beorn left the village that he had grown up in, a sense of loneliness came over him. He knew not what to do, so he began to drift toward the west. Deep in his heart he knew that he could not rest until he put himself before Princess Fairmina one more time. Her face was in his mind as clearly as a picture, and somehow he felt lighter and more joyful as he walked on—away from home and toward strangers.

12

Beorn and the Stranger

I fear you have made a grievous error, my son."

Balog could not meet his father's eyes. He'd been sitting alone outside his house, ignoring the cold, when Magon approached and spoke to him. Now Balog was flooded with a guilty feeling. "He ignored my commands!" he muttered. "I had no choice."

Magon came closer. "You and I have often disagreed, and many times you have been right, but this time I fear that you have gone against your own heart."

"What else was I do to? The whole village knew that I would have done worse to any other man. If he had not been my own son, he would have been killed."

"Ordinarily, my son, I think that your action might have been the right one, but I have been concerned about this whole matter."

"You've been against me from the very beginning."

"Only in this one thing," Magon said quickly. The snow was falling now in light, grainy flakes, but he did not pull up the hood of his parka, and the white flakes hardly showed against his silvery hair. He suddenly put a hand on Balog's shoulder. "And, my son," he said, "you have not been the same since you made that bargain with the wizard."

"I'm the same."

"No, you are not. Everyone has noticed, and I fear for you."

Indeed, Balog felt that there was some truth in what his father was saying. And he was secretly pleased with the weight of his father's hand. Just now he was feeling more alone than he had ever felt in his life. He had never been comfortable with his decision. And since visiting the palace of Zarkof, he'd been having bad dreams about the pale wizard. He glanced up and said, "I did what I thought was best for our people."

"I know you did, Son. You always do that. No one has ever questioned your loyalty."

"What else could I have done with Beorn? What would you have done if I had disobeyed *your* order?"

He knew the question put Magon in a hard place. His father had always been a strict man concerning the laws of the tribe. The silence ran on. Only the hissing of the snow across the ground and the keening of the wind around the side of the house could be heard.

Finally Magon said heavily, "I cannot help you now. But your wife and I both believe your decision to join the Dark Lord was hasty. As you know, we have both been followers of Goél for many years. We feel that his is the way of honor, and we were grieved when you chose to go with Goél's enemies."

Guilt shot through Balog, and he could only mutter, "I did what I thought was right." He got up and walked away quickly, unable to bear any more criticism. All his life he had respected his father. He also had put great trust in the insight of Olah. She had never pressured him to do anything, but there was gentle wisdom in her that he had often availed himself of. Now with these two both standing against him, he distrusted his own judgment.

"What am I going to do?" he asked himself. "Why do I feel so miserable?" He could not answer either question. After walking for what seemed hours, he went home, where he expected Olah to reproach him.

She said nothing, however. She merely set his meal before him.

"You're not eating. What's the matter? Are you sick?" Olah asked.

"I'm just not hungry."

She looked carefully into her husband's face. She always seemed to know when something was troubling him. Now as she filled his cup with hot tea, she said quietly, "You're worried about Beorn."

Balog was tormented. If he said yes, he was confessing that he had done the wrong thing. If he said no, that would be an outright lie. To cover his confusion he drank the tea and then said, "He'll be all right. He can take care of himself."

He got up then and went outside, unable to bear the eyes of his wife. He looked toward the west, where his son had disappeared. He had watched his father and Olah say good-bye to Beorn, and now he wished with all his heart that all of this had never happened.

"How did I get into this?" he muttered. "And how do I get out of it?"

The storm was unexpected. Beorn tried to ignore the snow, but it was coming down harder now. He shifted the bundle in which he bore his few possessions from one shoulder to the other.

Got to find shelter soon, he thought. *It's going to be bitter tonight.*

He made his way across the frozen ground, scarcely taking heed to which way his feet led him. Overhead the sky was slate gray, and he could barely see it for the snow that was now falling in large and downy flakes. On the ground before him a snow carpet was building up. His feet sank into it, and he regretted that he had forgotten to bring snowshoes.

It will soon be hard going if this doesn't let up.

But mostly his mind was not on the snow or on the cold but on his family. He had always loved and respected his father, and now there was a great wall between them. Beorn grieved over this, but, thinking on it, he said aloud, "What else could I have done? It would have been dishonorable to have killed the princess."

He realized then that he had spent much time of late thinking of her. Even as he plodded through the snow that was beginning to fall in long, slanting lines, he summoned up a picture of her face. He could see her long fair hair and her strange green eyes. Despite his plight, he felt a sudden burst of joy over what he had done. "No matter what happens to me, I saved her life. I'll have that even if I freeze to death out here."

For the next hour, the storm continued to build. The winds howled like a banshee, and Beorn leaned against the gale as a man would lean against a solid wall. It buffeted him, and his face was numb. His eyes burned from the fine, grainy snow that blew into them.

Got to find some place to get out of this. He looked around for an opening in a cliff, for a hollow tree, or for even a clump of trees that would offer shelter. But he could see nothing. He began to think seriously that this could indeed be the death of him. Many travelers had frozen in circumstances like this.

Beorn beat his cold hands together and stumbled on. He did not know how long he had walked, but he knew that he was tired and was moving slowly now. He dared not stop to rest, for he knew that would be the end.

Abruptly, a shadow appeared before him, and he did stop. His first thought was that he had been found by a polar bear or a saber-toothed tiger, but then a voice came out of the storm, saying, "Come this way."

Beorn staggered and would have fallen, but a strong hand came under his arm and supported him. He could not see his new companion's face. He was a tall man. At first he did not have presence of mind to think whether this was an enemy or a friend. But then he thought, *If he were an enemy, he would have killed me already. He must be a friend, although I don't recognize him.*

With a firm hand, the stranger led him to a snowy thicket where, among the trees, stood a small hut. The man stripped Beorn of his burden, said, "Quick, get inside!" and then left him.

Beorn fell to his hands and knees but managed to crawl into the hut. He had strength to do no more, and he huddled on the floor, shivering.

Soon the man was back, carrying a handful of twigs and some dead wood. He quickly kindled a fire by using flint and steel, and just the flickering of the red and yellow flames seemed to bring life into Beorn.

He held out his hands to the warmth as the smoke curled upward through the fireplace chimney. Being out of the wind was a blessing, and although he continued to shiver, the warmth that came from the fire soon brought feeling back to his hands. He beat them together and rubbed his face. Then he gave his close attention to the man who sat feeding small sticks into the flames.

"I thank you, stranger. I would have died, I think."

"You were in grave danger. I should think you would know better than to travel in weather like this, Beorn."

"You know my name? I don't think I know you, though." He looked closely at the man in the flickering light of the fire. But the stranger was wearing a heavy cloak with a hood that partially shaded his face. Beorn repeated, "I do not know you."

"No? We have met before. But you were only a child then when I visited your grandfather."

"My grandfather Magon?"

"I know him very well. I also know your mother and your father."

"May I have your name, sir?"

The stranger threw back the hood from his face. The cheekbones were high, and the eyes were deep-set under brown brows. There was strength in that face.

Beorn said, "I'm sorry. I cannot remember you."

"I am Goél."

A shock ran through Beorn. This was the fabled Goél of whom his grandfather and his mother had spoken for so many years? He could not speak for a moment, so great was the surprise in him. Finally he was able to say, "Now I do remember. You came to our village once. I was still small."

"You were six years old, and we had quite a talk together. You've probably forgotten, but we went for a long walk, and I told you several things."

Memory came back then, clearly. "I do remember now. I've thought of that time since then and spoken of it to my grandfather."

"Do you remember what I told you?"

"It's been so long ago . . ." Beorn muttered, thinking. The hut was growing warmer now, and he loosened his parka. "I remember you talked about honoring my parents."

"I did. You have a fine family, Beorn. Your father is

quick-tempered sometimes, but he is a good man. Few warriors are greater than he. And he chose a wife well. Olah, your mother, has been faithful."

"I do remember one other thing. It was the last thing you said, I believe." Beorn struggled with the memory that was indeed faint now. "I think I asked you how I could always be sure I was doing the right thing."

"You did." A smile turned the corners of Goél's lips upward. "I was surprised and pleased that so young a boy would ask such a thing. Do you remember what I said?"

"That I have never forgotten," Beorn said, smiling. "You said that if I did what pleased *you*, I would always be right."

"Exactly so. And I know, from talking to your grandfather, that you took that path well. You have been a good son, and you have been faithful to your grandfather, one of Goél's best servants."

Beorn could not believe this was happening. "But how did you find me? How did you know I would be here?"

Goél smiled, too. "I try to keep up with my servants and be sure they are safe."

"Then you know what happened—at home."

"Yes. I know."

"I could do nothing else, Goél. I didn't want to go against my father's orders but—"

"But you knew it would be wrong for Princess Fairmina to die."

"Yes!" Beorn said eagerly. "Exactly! I couldn't stand by and do nothing."

"You have a good heart, my son, and you have done the right thing. You pleased me."

"But I've offended my father."

Goél said quietly, "Your father is having a difficult time. Right now he needs you and your grandfather and your mother more than at any other time in his life. He is in grave danger of falling under the complete power of the Dark Lord. If that happens, he will be enslaved forever."

Beorn leaned forward. "That must not happen! I must do something."

"We must all do something, for I value your father. He has it in him to be one of the finest men alive, but he is just now being tested."

"What will I do? What can I do?"

"Where were you going when I found you, Beorn?"

"I don't know. I—I was lost."

"I think not," Goél said. "You had something in your heart."

Beorn could not meet Goél's eyes. He dropped his gaze to the fire and muttered, "Well, I did think I would go to see the princess and be sure she reached her home safely."

"And then what would you do?"

Confused, Beorn shrugged his shoulders. "I do not know," he admitted finally. "Everything is confused, and I'm unhappy."

"I think you should keep the counsel I gave you many years ago when you were a child."

Quickly Beorn looked up. "You mean—do what pleases you?"

"Exactly."

"But I do not know what to do. Tell me. Command me, and I will obey."

"Does this mean that you want to be the servant of Goél?"

At that moment, Beorn suddenly knew that what

130

his grandfather and his mother had spoken to him of Goél over the years had sunk deep into him. Subconsciously he had longed to meet this man and serve him. Now as he faced him across the flickering fire and saw the truth and love in Goél's eyes, he surrendered himself. "Yes, sire. I will serve you all the days of my life."

"I'm happy that you have made your decision."

"Command me. What shall I do?"

"Do what your heart has already told you. Go to the Lowami."

"But what shall I do when I get there? They will look upon me as the enemy."

"One thing the servants of Goél must learn, Beorn, is to trust me, to live by faith. Go to the tribe of Lowami and see the princess, and after that you will have to do what seems right. It could be dangerous, but I will protect you. There are hotheads among the Lowami as there are among the Yanti. Do not go as an enemy, for your whole purpose is to stop this senseless war. The enemy of the Yanti is not the Lowami. It is the Dark Lord. We must all unite against his terrible purpose. If the people do not unite, then they will be lost."

"I will do as you say, sire."

"Good. Now let us prepare a meal and sleep. And when morning comes, you will go to the village of the Lowami."

It was a night that Beorn never forgot. After eating a refreshing and heartening meal from Goél's supplies, they stayed up talking for a long time. They spoke of many things, and for the first time in his life Beorn knew that he had found a purpose for living. When he finally could stay awake no longer, he lay back, and the last thing he saw was Goél sitting before the fire, staring into it silently.

When Beorn awoke the next morning, Goél was gone. Disappointment came over him, but then he thought with joy, *But I will see him again. I know it.* He packed his few belongings, put his bundle on his shoulder, and left the hut with determination. He made straight across the snow toward the village of the Lowami.

13
The New Tribe Member

The return of Princess Fairmina came as a shock to Chief Denhelm. He and his wife were sitting in their house, silently grieving over her loss, when the door burst open and she appeared. Both jumped up, crying her name, and she flew to them.

The three of them stood in a tight embrace until finally Denhelm managed to get out the question, "How did you get here? What has happened, Daughter?"

"It is a long story—or maybe a short one," Fairmina said. She seemed exhausted and could barely speak.

"Here, Husband," Rimah said, "do not question her now. She is faint with weariness."

They quickly sat her down in a chair, and Rimah prepared a quick meal. Fairmina was obviously hungry. When she had finished eating, she drank a hot mixture of herbal tea that her mother forced on her.

"We had given you up, my daughter. We thought death had taken you," Denhelm said. He pulled up his chair as close as possible and held her hand. "Tell us, if you can, what happened."

Strengthened by the food, Fairmina related the story of her captivity. At the end she said, "And so I heard that the wizard had sent a message to kill me."

"How did you know this?" her mother asked. "Did they tell you?"

"Beorn told me."

"You speak often of this Beorn. He is the son of the Yanti chief?"

"Yes, and if it had not been for him, I do not know what I would have done," Fairmina said simply.

"He is not like his father, you say?" Rimah asked.

"His father is quick-tempered, while his son is very gentle—although a strong man and a great warrior."

"And he came and told you that Zarkof had ordered your death?"

"Yes. He had already taken me for a walk—as he did every day, to spare me the humiliation of the guards. He—he was very kind to me, Mother. The kindest man I've ever known—except for you, of course, Father."

"And what happened then?" Rimah asked.

"He took me out of my prison, but one guard was always with us. The most fearsome archer in all the tribe. There was no chance for escape. He would have put an arrow in me. But then Beorn told me of the order from Zarkof. And that his father would carry it out. And he said, 'You must get away.'"

"He said that? But that would be breaking his father's command."

"He knew that, Father, but he said it would be wrong for me to be executed."

Denhelm shook his head in wonder. "What happened then?"

"He overcame the guard and told me to run. The last I saw of him, he was holding the guard on the ground. Then I fled. They pursued, of course, but Beorn had given me instructions on how to avoid pursuit. And so I made it safely back to the village."

"A strange story." Denhelm shook his head once again. "I cannot believe it. That one of our enemy would become your friend."

"That's enough talk, Husband. Come, Fairmina.

You must go to bed. You are tired. You can tell us more after you have slept."

Denhelm sat waiting until his wife returned. "You think she is all right?"

"She's already asleep. She's very weary, but she'll be fine with a little rest." Rimah sat down and said, "What do you make of all this, Husband?"

"I do not know. I would have to say it was a miracle."

"Somehow I think that young man has qualities his father does not appreciate."

"I hope the chief did not have him beheaded for disobeying his orders. He sounds like too good a man to die like that."

"And did you note Fairmina's eyes when she spoke of him?"

"Her eyes? Well . . . no."

"You men are blind!" Rimah scoffed. "Could you not see how she admired him? It was as clear as day. It's no small wonder, either. He was the one that saved her life."

"We must have a council meeting and decide what all this means."

Denhelm called the council together at once, and the Seven Sleepers, along with the elders, listened as he related the story that Fairmina had told. When he ended, he said, "I cannot understand this except that I know this much—whatever the chief of the Yanti is, he has a son who is a man of honor."

The council talked for a time, and some were suspicious. One sour-faced elder said, "It's a trick! A trap of some kind! They let her go just to throw us off guard. We'd better double our precautions."

"Oh, you are always suspicious!" Denhelm said.

"Here we have my daughter back, and all you can think of is that there's something wrong about her deliverance."

The elder said no more, but his eyes were still filled with suspicion.

After the meeting, the Sleepers had a meeting of their own. Mat, as usual, said, "There's something wrong with all this. I don't trust them. Not one inch!"

But Tam grinned cheerfully. "You'd complain if they hung you with new rope, Mat. We have the princess back safe and sound, and you're doing nothing but complaining."

"I'm a realist. You're an idealist."

"If that means," Tam said, "that you're always griping and complaining and I'm always looking at the good side, I'm glad to hear it!"

"Isn't it the most romantic thing you ever heard?"

Reb groaned and looked at Abbey.

Her eyes were bright as stars. "I wonder what he looks like."

He groaned again.

Josh winked at Sarah, sitting across from him. "Probably fifty years old and fat and dumpy."

"No," Abbey said dreamily, "he's tall and handsome and has good manners! I just know it."

"Well, I don't care what he looks like," Sarah said. "I'm just relieved that the princess is back. I must admit my faith was pretty small."

"No wonder," Reb said. "Those Yanti are rough. They could have sent her head back in a sack."

"Don't say things like that!" Wash said. "It makes chills go all over me."

Reb Jackson grinned. "Chills have been going all

136

over you since we got to Whiteland. You're just cold. That's all."

When the meeting broke up, Reb found himself alone with Abbey, and he teased her a little. "You're always seeing some kind of romance in everything that happens, Abbey."

"I can't help it. That's just the way I am."

"Oh, I'm not fussing about it," Reb said. "I think that's fine. I'm kind of romantic myself."

"You romantic! Don't be foolish!"

"Well, I am! Why, one time I read a romance novel."

"I've read a thousand of them."

"Well, once I read one, I thought I was done. They're all alike, aren't they?"

"Maybe they are, but if you like a good romance, it doesn't matter if the same thing happens over and over."

"It looks like you could just keep the same book and read it over and over and save all that money."

"What did you read when you were back in Oldworld?"

"Westerns."

"Well, I heard someone say there were only seven plots for all the Westerns ever written."

Reb took off his Stetson and scratched his sandy hair. "That's about right. The rustlers robbing the ranchers . . ."

"Then why did you keep on reading them?" Abbey laughed. "You're as bad as I am."

"I guess so. Anyway," Reb said, "we're going to have to be a little bit romantic to get out of this."

"Do you think we'll ever see the man who saved the princess?"

"Doubt it. He's not likely to come visiting."

Reb remembered his words the next day. He heard a shout and popped his head out of the igloo. "Hey, look! They've caught somebody!" He scrambled out and was followed by Dave, Jake, and Wash.

"There's Josh. Who's that fellow they've got?"

Abbey and Sarah came out of their igloo as well. Abbey said, "Who's that with Josh? Isn't he handsome!"

"I don't think I ever saw him before," Sarah said. "Let's go find out."

When the others ran up, Josh said, "You're not going to believe this, but this is Beorn, the son of Chief Balog of the Yantis. Beorn, this is Abbey and Sarah and . . ." He named off the boys.

Beorn was not bound, but he was being guarded by several Lowami warriors, who watched him closely. He bowed gracefully and said, "I am happy to know you, ladies—and all."

Abbey's eyes grew big. "You're the one who saved the princess?"

A flush came to Beorn's cheeks. "I came to see if she had arrived home safely."

"Oh, yes," Sarah said quickly. "She has. She was very tired when she got back, but she's probably up by now. I want to thank you very much. She's become a very good friend of mine. It was wonderful of you to come to her aid."

"It was something I had to do."

"Enough talk!" the guards said. "You must face the chief."

No one was about to leave, and by the time the prisoner stood in front of the house of Chief Denhelm, practically everyone in the village was there. The door opened, and the chief stepped out, followed by his wife.

"We've taken a captive, sire," one of the guards reported. "This is one of our enemies. We caught him approaching our village."

"What is your name?" Denhelm asked.

"My name is Beorn. I am the son of Chief Balog."

"And how is it that you come into your enemies' hands?"

Beorn had no chance to answer for at that moment the door opened again, and Princess Fairmina appeared. She took one look and then let out a glad cry. "Beorn!" She flew across the ground and put out her hands. They were taken at once by Beorn, and she cried in delight, "I'm so glad to see you!"

"I came, Princess, to be sure you arrived safely at home."

"I was so afraid for you," Fairmina said. "I was afraid something awful would happen to you for letting me go."

Beorn laughed softly. "I was in some danger of that, but my grandfather and my mother persuaded my father to let me live." He looked around. "But he drove me out of the village, so I have no home now."

Denhelm advanced. He put his hand on the young man's shoulder. He said warmly, "My daughter has told us how you saved her life and how you showed her courtesy. I invite you to make your home with us."

Total silence fell over the crowd. To invite a Yanti to become one of them—this was unheard of!

Then Rimah came forward and put out her hand. Her eyes were glowing. "We welcome you into our midst, Beorn. And I thank you for giving us our daughter's life."

Chief Balog's son seemed to have expected anything but this. He looked into the eyes of Rimah, then into the noble face of Denhelm, and finally into the eyes of Fairmina. "It gives me great honor to accept your invitation, Chief Denhelm."

Rimah said at once, "Can we not hear a cheer for the new member of our tribe?"

A ragged cheer went up, and Abbey's voice could be heard above all the rest.

"We must celebrate," the chief said. "Not only my daughter's return but the coming of the one who made it possible."

The feast was something to remember. There was plenty to eat and much merrymaking. Beorn and Fairmina sat together to the left of the chief.

Josh, seated beside Sarah, said, "Look at those two. She can't take her eyes off him."

Sarah had been watching. "I hate to admit it, but this time Abbey was right. It *is* romantic. Just like something out of a book."

"Sounds like you've already got them married."

"Of course they'll get married. Don't you see how he looks at her and how she looks at him?"

"How am I supposed to know by a look what's going on? He may already have a sweetheart back among his people."

"Don't be silly. If he had, he wouldn't be looking at her like that!" Sarah scoffed.

Josh suddenly laughed. "You're as bad as Abbey. I guess all girls are sappy when it comes to romances."

Sarah glared at him. "Sappy! That's what you think of me? Well, I appreciate your kind remarks!"

"Wait a minute, Sarah! I didn't mean sappy."

"What did you mean?"

"I meant . . . well . . . I guess I meant . . . well, *romantic.*"

"That's a little better," she said. "And it wouldn't hurt you to have a little romance in your soul."

"Who, me?"

"Yes, you! Who do you think I'm talking to?"

Josh eyed Sarah. "How do we get into these arguments?"

"Because you don't have any romance in your soul. That's why."

Josh had no answer for this, so he turned to talk to Jake Garfield, who was on the other side of him.

Jake was busy eating, but he had heard the conversation. "Give up on her, Josh," he said loudly. "You've got no romance in your soul." He laughed when Sarah made a face at him. "Well, it's turning out pretty good, isn't it?"

"Good? Have you forgotten those ice wraiths and that we're in a war?" Josh asked. "You can talk about romance all you want to, but we're still in a mess."

After the celebration meal, Fairmina said, "Would you like to see our village, Beorn?"

"I would like that very much."

"Come, then. I will show you."

There was really not much to see in the village, but Beorn spoke glowingly of it and that pleased her. He said, "It's very much like my own village."

"Is it? I suppose so." She walked along slowly for a while. "What will happen with you and your father?"

"I cannot say."

"I am surprised that you came here. You risked your life, you know."

"I suppose that is true." He hesitated, then turned to face her. "But I met someone on my way here."

"Who was that?"

Beorn related quickly how he'd gotten lost in the snowstorm, and then he said, "I was about to freeze to death, when suddenly a man came out of the night."

"But who was it?" she asked again.

"I thought it was an enemy at first, but it was Goél."

"Goél! *He* came to you?"

"Yes." And Beorn told her of how they had talked long into the night. "He encouraged me to please him— to do what is right."

Dropping her gaze, Fairmina said, "And what does your heart tell you is right, Beorn?"

He said quietly, "My heart tells me that I have never seen one as fair as the Princess Fairmina. And that I will love her all the days of my life."

Fairmina felt her face flush.

"I wanted you to know how I felt. You may never feel anything for me—"

"But I do, Beorn! How could I fail to admire you when you risked everything to save me?"

"That is enough for now," he said. "Show me the rest of your village."

"What would you say, Husband, if Beorn asked to marry Fairmina?" Rimah asked one afternoon.

"What would *you* say?"

"I would say that I see honor and love in him."

"But he is a Yanti."

"That matters not to me as long as he has honor."

Denhelm thought of this much, but he also kept thinking of the danger that lay over his people.

"My wife seems to have forgotten that we are living on the edge of death here," he said to Josh one day. The two were standing on the bank, fishing through a hole in the ice.

"I think we must do something, sire. You are right. It is just a matter of time before the ice wraiths come again. The pale wizard is a servant of the Dark Lord. And I can tell you from experience," he said grimly, "the Dark Lord never gives up. He will have us all as slaves, or he will have our death."

"You are wise beyond your years, Josh. But what to do?"

"Could we have one more council? Perhaps Goél will come, or perhaps he will give us wisdom in the strange way that he has."

Denhelm followed Josh's suggestion, and that evening the Long House was filled. Even Volka, who never said a single word during a council meeting, was sitting with his back against the wall, taking it all in. Beside him sat Mat and Tam, and the Sleepers were arranged alongside them.

The chief called the meeting to order. "We are grateful for our daughter's return, but we must not forget that we are in grave danger here."

Fairmina spoke up. "You are right, Father. While I was a captive, I heard much talk of their using the ice wraiths again."

"That is true, Chief Denhelm." The speaker was Beorn. To his apparent shock and amazement, he had been asked to attend the council. "My father," he said, "has made a foolish commitment to the pale wizard, and you know that Zarkof is in the service of the Dark Lord. I heard that, as soon as new riders are trained to control the ice wraiths, a raid will come that could destroy all of the Lowami. That could come at any time."

There was much talk, but no one knew exactly what to do.

Beorn said no more. Perhaps he thought speaking would be out of place, but finally Fairmina, who had been studying him, said, "There is something on your heart, is there not, Beorn?"

"Yes. There is something, but I hesitate to speak it."

"Speak freely," Denhelm said. "What is it?"

"I once made a visit to the White Palace—the fortress of the pale wizard." He described his visit there with his father. He told of the monster Shivea, and a shudder seemed to go over everyone present. "I've never seen anything like her, and she guards the pale wizard's great secret."

"Secret? What is his secret?" Denhelm asked in a puzzled tone.

"There is a crystal chair that sits underneath his palace. It is in a large cavern—the only thing there—and it is through the chair that the Dark Lord gives his commands and his power to Zarkof."

"What is it like?"

"It looks like glass, but it glows with an evil glow. And when Zarkof sits in it, he hears the Dark Lord's voice and his whole body is filled with the same ominous glow. It is frightening to see."

"This chair. You think somehow it is the key to the power of the wizard?"

Slowly Beorn nodded. "I have thought of it ever since I was there. He guards it so well that it must be the secret to his power."

"Then if the chair were destroyed," Fairmina said,

"the wizard would be destroyed as far as having any power is concerned."

"I think that is true, but it is better guarded than you can imagine." Beorn went on to describe the palace. "There is only one entrance, and it is guarded day and night. There are many twisting corridors. If one did not know the way, he could wander for days."

"But you have been there. You could find your way, could you not?" Fairmina asked.

"Well, I've tried to keep it in my memory. I *think* I could find my way to the room where the chair is. But you are forgetting Shivea, the monster spider."

Silence fell over the group, and at last Denhelm said, "We must think much of this."

"I wish," Beorn said quietly, "that Goél would come."

"We all wish that," Denhelm said. "But until he does, we must act as men." He looked at his daughter and smiled. "And as women. We will speak no more just now, but we must make a decision promptly. I will call another meeting when I have made up my mind as to what to do."

14

The Gifts of Goél

It seems pretty plain to me," Jake said. He was standing in the midst of the other Sleepers, who were slumped around listening. The most outspoken of the Seven Sleepers, he had just concluded a long fiery speech on what had to be done.

"We've got to destroy that chair."

"Oh, brilliant, Jake! Brilliant!" Dave said. "Why couldn't I understand that?" He groaned and rolled over on his mattress of furs. "How did we ever get along without you?"

"What's wrong?" Jake demanded. "It's pretty clear, isn't it? We get rid of the chair, we get rid of the wizard."

"Maybe," Josh said. "We don't even know that for sure."

Jake nodded his head firmly. "Beorn says so."

"But even if that's true," Sarah spoke up, "how in the world would anyone ever get to that chair?"

"We've had to do things as hard as this before," Jake argued.

"I'm not even sure about that," Josh said. "It sounds like one of the worst jobs that anybody could take on."

"Don't you remember when we had to get through to the tower of the Dark Lord on our first quest?" Jake said. "We got that done, didn't we?"

"But we had the advice of Goél that time," Josh said wearily. After the council meeting, they had

147

argued half the night about what to do. He was tired of the whole thing. "I just don't know what to do."

"And do I find you again wondering what to do?" a voice suddenly said.

And there stood Goél!

The Sleepers all jumped up and surrounded him.

"Goél!" Josh cried happily. "You're here!"

"Yes, I'm here and glad to see you again, my young friends."

"Can we give you something to eat?" Sarah asked.

"No, my Sarah." He smiled. "You're always serving others. Why don't you all sit down, and you can tell me of your problems." His smile widened. "You always have problems."

They sat here and there on the furs, and Josh started in. "I expect you already know about our main problem. Beorn told us how you met him in the storm and saved his life."

"He told us about the chair too," Jake said. "I've been trying to get everyone to see all we have to do is get to that chair."

Goél listened as Jake made an eloquent plea for destroying the chair. He listened while the others argued how difficult or even impossible that would be. Finally the Sleepers fell silent and just sat looking at him.

"In every battle there comes one single moment on which success or failure rests," he began. "Perhaps it is just one blow of the sword, but if that blow is not made, then the man will be lost, then his part of the army will be lost, then the entire army will be lost, and then the war will be lost." After Goél let his words sink in, he said, "I think now that one thing is clear. Jake is right. The chair must be destroyed."

148

"Couldn't you destroy it yourself?" Dave asked. "I mean, after all, it would be easy for you."

"Dave, you are tired, or you would not speak so. Have you learned nothing?" There was sadness in Goél's eyes. "Have you not yet learned that usually my purposes must be accomplished by others?"

Dave shook his head. "But I don't understand, sire. You have the power to do it—all by yourself."

"This world is not made up only of Goél but of many peoples. You Sleepers have been sent from a long distance, from another time, to help men and women and young people here control their own destinies. If I were to step in and solve all their problems, what would that do for their growth—or yours? Nothing."

Josh studied Goél's face. "You're telling us that we have to do this ourselves, aren't you?"

"I'm afraid so, but it is through the hard things that men and women learn. Not the easy things."

"You've said this so often, Goél," Sarah said, "but this seems like an *impossible* thing."

"It may be impossible to most people, but you are the Seven Sleepers, and I have chosen you. You will have my help."

Josh hesitated. "Are you telling us that we must destroy the chair?"

"That is your decision to make, but that is my counsel."

"But can we do it?" Reb asked. "I mean, that sounds pretty tough."

"Is this Reb speaking, who has slain dragons? After all you have gone through, Reb, do you still doubt me?"

"No, I really don't, sire." Reb's jaw tightened, and he grinned. "With your help, just let me at that overgrown spider. I'll drop a rope over her head and bull-dog her just like I would a steer back home."

"That's my Reb speaking." Goél laughed aloud, and a light came to his eyes.

Josh said, "Well, it all seems easy enough with you standing here with us, but we'll be all alone under that ice castle."

"I would have you do this for your own sake. You will take with you Princess Fairmina and Beorn, son of Balog. Go get them now, so that they too may hear my instructions."

Fifteen minutes later, Reb returned with the princess and Beorn.

Beorn at once fell to his knees before Goél. "Sire," he said, "your servant forever."

"Rise," said Goél. "You are a faithful servant of Goél. And you, my daughter. Will you serve me as well?"

"Yes, Goél. I will try to serve you as well as my father and my mother."

"Then you will serve me well indeed," he said warmly. "Now, listen carefully. This war will never be won by armies. Both tribes will be destroyed if the Dark Lord has his way. The Yanti will destroy the Lowami. And the Yanti will be enslaved to the Dark Lord himself under the hand of Zarkof. So the chair must be destroyed and the wizard's power broken. This is the company I have chosen to carry out that mission. The Sleepers will go, and you two will go with them."

"What about us?" Mat and Tam spoke up at the same time.

Goél said, "You will not go on this adventure. Nor will you, my friend Volka."

150

He ignored their protests and turned back to Beorn and the princess. "Now, I have two gifts to give you." He handed Princess Fairmina a small glass vial. It contained some sort of fluid that changed color constantly. "When your enemy would triumph, hold this high. It will render him unable to see you and your companions."

"That will be most useful, sire," Fairmina said.

"And this I give to you, my son." From under his flowing robe, Goél produced a sword. He drew it out of its sheath, and it glittered as if it had a light of its own. "This sword is like no other. Among other abilities, it is the weapon that can slay the monster Shivea. Take it, and use it well."

Reverently Beorn took the sword by the hilt. He stared at it for a moment, then his eyes met those of Goél. "I will obey your command, sire."

Goél looked about the group once more and said, "You must go at once."

"Must I not tell my father?" Fairmina asked.

"No. This mission is not for him. It is your quest, so go quickly. And remember that—in the darkest hour —I, Goél, will be with you."

15

The White Palace

The snowstorm that had trapped and almost killed Beorn was still sweeping across the land. Beorn led the company of Sleepers through it, for he best knew the countryside. After difficult travel, they neared the border between the Lowami and the Yanti tribes. At that point he called a halt. "We must save our strength," he said.

"How can we rest in this storm?" Fairmina had to lift her voice to be heard above the screaming wind.

"I know this land well. There is a cave not far from here to give us shelter. Some supplies should be there. Our people use it from time to time when a storm catches them away from the village."

"Let us find it quickly then," Fairmina said. "This cold sucks the strength even from my bones, and the Sleepers cannot stand it. They are not bred to it as we are."

Fairmina had spoken the truth, for the cold had penetrated Josh's warm furs and insulated underwear. Cold seemed to reach its icy fingers down into his bones too. He noticed that Sarah was pale and her lips were pursed tightly together.

"Are you all right, Sarah?"

"As all right as I can be in this terrible cold."

Beorn led them toward the sheer face of a cliff. "This way. It's not far."

They followed him for perhaps two hundred yards, and then he stopped, saying with relief, "We're here. Get inside—quickly."

The Sleepers stumbled into the cave. It was dark, but Beorn struck a light from flint and soon had a small fire going. He kept feeding it from the firewood that had been stacked there.

"We keep several places like this stocked with firewood and food in case someone gets trapped out. We can make some hot broth."

The Sleepers all gathered around the fire, soaking up the warmth, while Fairmina took care of the cooking. She found a large pot and chunks of frozen meat, and the smell of hot stew soon filled the cavern.

When it was ready, she said, "We'll have to take turns with the vessels. There aren't enough to go around."

Reb said, "I brought me a plate. I wasn't taking any chances."

It turned out that the rest of the Sleepers also were carrying their eating ware, and soon all were taking the delicious stew onto their plates.

"Best stew I ever had," Reb said. "It's even better than the black bug stew I used to eat back in Arkansas."

"Black bug stew! You eat the awfulest things, Reb!" Abbey said.

Fairmina smiled. "Black bug stew does sound a little awful. What is it?"

"Well, it's not really made out of bugs," Reb said. "But we'd be camping out in the dark beside the river, and I'd be cooking something—and sometimes a big black bug would fly into it. It'd be too dark to see it, so it just kind of got mixed up with the rest of the stew. Maybe gave it a little extra flavor." He nudged Abbey, who had wrinkled up her nose. "Maybe I could find a bug to put in your stew, Abbey."

"Don't you dare!" she warned. "This is good just as it is!"

"It's a good thing you knew about this cave, Beorn," Josh said. "I don't think we could have made it much farther."

"This is a hard land," Beorn said. "We have to make provision for trouble. Getting ready for winter is just about like getting ready for war with the enemy. You store up supplies like this for those who get caught out in bad weather. People have to have plenty of food to last when they're snowed in."

"It's a tough land, all right," Dave said. "I don't see how you live here all the time."

"It's very different from where you came from, I suppose," Beorn said.

This set the Sleepers to talking about their homes back in Oldworld.

"And I suppose all that's gone forever," Fairmina put in.

"It is," Josh said, "but I'm believing that Goél will make a better world someday. That's what he says."

"I too believe he will." Beorn nodded. Then he must have noticed the weariness on everyone's face, for he said, "And now let's all get some rest."

The Sleepers fell into their furs and instantly were asleep, exhausted by their journey. Only Beorn and Fairmina sat by the fire for a time.

Suddenly he said, "Are you warm enough?" He reached for a fur and put it around her shoulders.

Surprised, she looked up. "People usually don't take care of me like that. I take care of myself."

"You're a strong woman, Fairmina."

She seemed embarrassed. After a pause she said, "The other girls of our tribe know how to talk to men."

"It is the same with us. But you never learned, is that it?"

"No," Fairmina said quietly. "I knew I would have to take my father's place, and so I had no time for the young men who came."

"That's a shame. You were robbing one of them of a great treasure."

She didn't answer. Perhaps she was struggling with her thoughts.

"Now, you must rest, also."

"Do you think we have a chance to succeed in this mission?" she asked, standing and gathering up her furs.

"There is always a chance of success to those who are in the service of Goél."

But for a long time Beorn lay awake, thinking about the future. He alone had seen the fortress that they must penetrate. He alone had seen the awful Shivea and knew how deadly she was. Even the wizard feared her—and he had the medallion that kept her from attacking.

Finally Beorn murmured under his breath, "Goél, this is impossible except with your help. But I'm believing that you will find a way to help us all."

"There it is," Beorn said quietly. "The White Palace of the pale wizard."

The Sleepers stood gaping at the sheer walls that rose in front of them. Josh could see barred windows and wondered what sort of prisoners were kept behind them.

"Is there only the one gate?" Fairmina asked.

"So the wizard said. And it is well guarded."

Josh was standing beside Beorn, his eyes searching the fortress. "It looks impossible, Beorn."

"It will be difficult. There may be as many as twenty guards inside the gate. They expect an attack from nowhere else."

The group fell silent, and Josh shivered.

"Well, the gate must be attempted," Beorn said. "We will do what warriors can do. If we perish, we perish."

"No, wait!" Everyone turned to look at Dave, who had an odd look on his face. "I just had a thought."

"What is it, Dave?" Fairmina said. "Surely there's no other way except to attack the gate."

"But that's exactly what they're expecting." He appeared to be thinking hard. "If we can get inside another way . . ."

"But there *is* no other way," Beorn repeated. "This is the only opening."

"It may be the only opening on this level," Dave said, "but there are other openings." He pointed upward. "There are windows all the way up."

"They're all barred," Beorn protested.

"Not at the very top," Dave said.

"That's the *wizard's* dwelling."

"It may be, but there are no bars on the windows —that I can see."

Josh, who had the keenest eyes of any of the Sleepers, tilted his head back. "You're right, Dave!" he exclaimed. "There are no bars on those upper windows."

"Then his idea is right," Jake said. "Our only hope is to get in that way."

"I wish one of us was a bird," Wash said. "We could just fly up."

Beorn kept on looking upward. "No one could

climb those walls. They go straight up, and there's no place to get a handhold."

"What are you thinking, Dave?" Sarah asked. "Do you have a plan?"

"I had a hobby back in Oldworld."

"Like collecting stamps? What good is that?" Reb asked.

"No. I was into mountain climbing—rappeling and things like that."

Josh motioned toward the White Palace. "But you couldn't climb that!"

"I don't know whether I can or not, but it looks to me as if I've got to try."

An exclamation of surprise went around the group, and Fairmina cried, "Only a fly could climb that wall!"

"Well, there was once a climber called the human fly," Dave said. "I read a book about him. A climb like this may not be impossible."

"That first window is at least twenty feet up," Josh argued. "Even if you could get up to it, what would you do then?"

"Go up to the next window. They're right over each other."

Josh eyed the windows. They were not staggered. One was directly above another.

"Look," Dave said, frowning as he thought. "If we could rig up some kind of grappling hook . . ."

"What's a grappling hook?" Beorn asked with puzzlement on his brow.

"It's sort of a three-pronged hook. You tie it on the end of a rope, and you throw it up. One of the hooks catches, and then you pull yourself up."

"I've seen those things," Josh said. "But I don't know how we'd make one."

Jake said, "Well, I'm the inventor here. Let me see what I can come up with."

Jake always carried an assortment of tools and supplies in his backpack. That made the pack very heavy, and the Sleepers were continually teasing him about it.

But now Josh said, "Jake, if you can come up with something like that, you're a genius."

Jake set to work. The others moved around, waiting and, for the most part, just looking at the forbidding heights.

Fairmina asked Sarah, "Do you think it can be done?"

"Jake's pretty smart about things like this."

But Beorn said, "Even so, could *anyone* go up that wall?" He shuddered. "I wouldn't be able to do it."

Sarah said, "I don't know, but it does seem the only way."

Jake found some metal pieces in his kit, and with pliers he fashioned them into hooks. He also carried some of the rawhide that the Lowamis used for rope. He bound the pieces together, making a triple hook. Then he sharpened the ends, and finally he held up his invention. "Well, there it is."

"Let me see." Dave took the grappling hook and pulled at it. "It's strong enough," he said. "I think it'll hold my weight. Maybe not yours, Beorn, but mine."

"But what will you do with it?" Beorn asked with puzzlement.

"I'll attach a rope, then throw it up and hope it catches on the first window ledge. Then I climb up to that window, stand on the ledge there, throw it up to the next, and climb up to that. That way I get all the way to the top. At least," Dave said slowly, with a careful look at the sheer height of the White Palace, "that's the way it should work."

"Dave, you'll kill yourself trying that," Sarah said. "It can't be done."

All the Sleepers knew that Dave Cooper had not always been the best. He had even betrayed them once. Now he said, "I let you down once, and maybe this is my chance to make up for that. Let's tie the best knot you can onto this grappling hook, Jake."

As everyone watched, Jake attached a strip of rawhide rope. "I don't know how strong this is," he said. "If it breaks, you're a goner."

Dave managed to grin. "I've climbed worse than this in Switzerland. My dad took me there. We went up some pretty sheer slopes. Anyway, we've got to do it."

"What will you do when you do get to the top?" Beorn asked. "You'll be inside, and the rest of us will be out here."

"I'll have to play it by ear. All of you stay by the gate. If I make it, I'll go down and see if I can draw the guards away. If I do, I'll open the gate."

Dave took the grappling hook and then drew a deep breath. "Wish me luck," he said.

Abbey put a hand on his arm. "Be careful, Dave. I couldn't stand it if anything happened to you."

Dave patted her on the shoulder. "I'll do my best. And when you all get in, be careful. It's going to be pretty hairy."

Josh and the others watched Dave approach the wall. There were no guards outside, and Beorn said, "They don't really need any. But someone may see him if he gets to that first window."

They looked on as Dave positioned himself and made a coil of the rope. He seemed to measure the distance, and then he threw up the grappling hook. It sailed high in the air, but fell a foot wide of the mark.

Josh groaned. "He missed."

But on the second try, the grappling hook caught. "He's got it!" Reb whispered. "And look at him go up that rope—just like a circus acrobat."

Josh could see that, indeed, Dave's mountain climbing skill was coming in handy. He climbed hand over hand, until he reached the first window. Then he took hold of one of the bars and pulled himself up onto the ledge. It was a large window, and Josh half expected a big hand to grab Dave or a spear to fly out and kill him.

But Dave waved, rewound his rope, estimated the distance, and threw again.

"So far so good," Wash said. "Ooh, look at him go! I wouldn't do that for a million dollars."

"I'll bet he wouldn't, either," Abbey said. "He's doing it for us."

Dave went up, stage by perilous stage. Several times his grappling hook missed, and he had to try again and again.

And then Beorn whispered, "He's at the last barred window. If he can do it one more time, he'll be at the wizard's rooms."

"What if the wizard is there?" Josh said. "What then?"

"Then it's all up with us. No way he could stand against the pale wizard."

Breathlessly Josh saw Dave make the last cast. The grappling hook caught, he gave them one wave, made the sign of victory, and went up the rope. He reached the top, pulled himself onto the window ledge, and then disappeared inside.

"Well, he's in," Sarah said. "At least he did what he set out to do."

"Let's get over close to the gate. If it opens," Josh said, "it won't be open long."

He actually thought there was little hope that Dave would be able to draw the guards away.

Hurriedly they crossed the clearing toward the palace. Josh desperately hoped that no one would see them. But all stayed quiet, and they stationed themselves on each side of the gate, where no one could see through the bars.

With his back pressed against the cold, hard stone, Josh turned to look at Sarah. "Here we are again," he whispered.

"Yes. Seems like we've been here before."

"Do you think we can make it, Sarah?"

"We've got to trust Goél."

Josh kept himself pressed against the wall. The wait seemed unending. He imagined all kinds of things —that Dave had been caught, that he was already in a torture chamber, that he was dead . . .

Then suddenly the gate swung open, and Dave leaped out. "Come!" he called softly.

Beorn and Fairmina darted through the opening, followed by Josh and the other Sleepers.

"Where are the guards?" Josh asked.

"I made a big racket down the hall and then dodged around. But they'll be back, so let's move fast. We must get down to the lower level."

Even at that moment six guards appeared, and a yell went up.

"We'll fight our way through!" Beorn said.

All swords were drawn, but it was the archery of Fairmina and Sarah that saved them. Moving like lightning, the girls shot two arrows apiece that silenced four of the guards. The other two, outnumbered, turned and ran.

"We've been found out now, but if we can get to the chair, we'll be all right," Beorn said. "Follow me!"

Zarkof was spending the day not in his chambers but in a lower level of the palace, working in a laboratory that he used at times.

Suddenly, a guard burst in. "Sire, enemies have entered the castle!"

Zarkof knew who the enemy had to be. "The Sleepers!" he gasped. He also knew that his life lay in the balance. "If they are not killed, I will execute every one of you! Destroy them all!"

"Yes, sire. The guard has been called out."

Zarkof grabbed his sword and flew down the stairs. *They're here to destroy me*, he thought. *And they're here to destroy the chair.* When he got to the very lowest level, he ran through a secret corridor. At its end he loosed a bolt, and Shivea was free from her confinement.

"Now," he said, "you may kill, and you may eat!" He held up the medallion, or she would have killed and eaten him. "There is other prey for you, my dear. Destroy all that approach the chair!"

Shivea's eyes glowed, and her claws scrabbled on the stone floor as she disappeared down the passage.

"That should take care of them. No one has ever defeated Shivea."

"Quick! This way!" Beorn led Josh and his companions along a maze of corridors and down a twisting stair to the lowest level.

There they came upon a large body of guards, well armed. The battle that took place was too close for archery work, so it had to be swords. There was the sound of clashing steel, and for a while it appeared that they would be overwhelmed.

But then Fairmina seemed to suddenly remember the gift of Goél. As they were being pressed back and death was imminent, she held up the vial and called out, "Goél! Goél, come to our aid!"

The vial in her hand emitted a pale amber light, and the soldiers of the wizard grabbed at their eyes.

"What's happening?" one of them yelled. "I can't see anybody! Where did they go?"

"They can't see us," Beorn said. "Now act!"

"This'll be easy!" Reb yelled. "Get 'em all!"

But the sound of voices without bodies and the threat of invisible enemies were too much for the guards. They turned and fled.

Immediately Beorn said, "This way." He led them quickly along two more corridors to a black iron gate. "This will take us to the chair."

"And is this where the monster is? Shivea?" Dave asked.

"Yes. We'll have to pass through several more corridors, and she could be anywhere."

He unbarred the gate and took a deep breath. "But we are trapped here. We either find the chair and destroy it, or else we ourselves will die."

Then Beorn threw himself into the corridor beyond the iron gate, and the others followed him.

Josh brought up the rear to be sure there were no stragglers. He muttered to Reb, "Keep your sword out. Sounds like that monster Shivea may be harder to handle than any dragon you ever faced."

16

The Crystal Chair

The stones in the walls that Beorn had noticed on his first visit illuminated their way. He warned everyone to search for signs of Shivea.

"What are these rocks?" Jake asked. "They glow like light bulbs."

"Probably some of Zarkof's evil wizardry," Fairmina said. She held her bow ready in her left hand and had an arrow notched.

They made several turns, and then Beorn announced, "We've made it. There's the door at the far end of this corridor. The crystal chair is behind it."

But just then there was a scrabbling sound, and Josh cried, "Look out! There she is!"

And there she was. Shivea. Her eyes were red, and she towered over their heads, making a monstrous shape. Poison dripped from her fangs. Raising two of her spider arms with their razor-sharp claws, she advanced slowly toward them.

"Spread out! Don't get in a group!" Beorn yelled.

Without hesitation Fairmina drew her bow and sent an arrow at the beast. Josh saw to his dismay that it merely glanced off. *Shivea must have some kind of armored hide*, he thought.

Quickly Fairmina shot arrow after arrow. Sarah did the same. None of them seemed to affect Shivea.

Then Beorn held up the sword that Goél had given him. Raising it high, he ran straight at the monster spider.

"Don't!" Fairmina cried. She dropped her bow and arrow and pulled her own sword and followed.

Shivea reached out for Beorn with her claws, but with a mighty swing of Goél's sword, he cut off one leg. The monster emitted a terrible scream and leaped at him.

"She's got him! He's underneath her!" Jake yelled. "Come on, everybody! We have to help!"

The Sleepers and Fairmina ran at the spider, slashing at her legs. But Shivea was concerned only with the one underneath her.

At that moment a laugh filled the chamber. "So. This is the end of the Seven Sleepers!"

Josh whirled to see the wizard, stepping out from a hidden door.

Zarkof laughed again. "The Dark Lord will be pleased that all of the Sleepers die together. You will be a fine meal for my pet spider. Kill them all, Shivea!" he ordered.

The wizard advanced. But as he did so, perhaps the spider had some dim memory of how this man had tormented her. In any case, she turned away from the prey who lay under her and moved toward Zarkof.

Fear leaped into his eyes. He grabbed for the medallion on his chest.

But Josh was faster. He guessed that the medallion had something to do with the wizard's control of Shivea. With a cry, he threw himself at Zarkof. He ripped the medallion from the wizard's neck, breaking the chain.

"Give me that!" Zarkof screamed, clutching at him.

But Reb seized one of the wizard's arms. Dave seized the other, setting Josh free and pushing Zarkof away. And then Shivea was upon them.

Zarkof let out a scream and tried to flee. But he was too late. The claw of the monster reached out and closed on his throat.

Beorn staggered to his feet. "Run! She'll kill us all!" he yelled. Then he threw himself between the spider's legs. In his hand Goél's sword glowed in the semidarkness. He thrust the blade upward, shouting, "For Goél!"

A terrible roaring filled the chamber, and Shivea flung herself to one side. Her legs clawed the air as, again and again, Beorn thrust into her body the sword that had been the gift of Goél.

Josh ran up to his friend. "You've done it, Beorn! She's dead!" He could hardly stand the stench of the monster. "Come away."

And then Fairmina came to support Beorn on the other side. "Please come, Beorn. Our task is not over yet."

"I know. The chair," he gasped, still gripping the great sword. He had to be supported by Fairmina and Josh, but he led them to the secret door.

"Open it," he told Josh. "Just hold out the medallion."

And then many footsteps sounded in the corridor above.

"Everybody inside—and close the door behind us!" Beorn cried.

Wash and Reb slammed the door and put their backs against it. "They can't get in. We've got the medallion," Reb said. "We'll have to hold 'em if they try to break down the door."

But Josh stood staring at the chair that he had heard so much about. It appeared to be made of glass, and it glowed with an evil light. Then he ran toward it.

"We've got to destroy this thing!" he cried, and he

brought down his sword on the chair. But the blade rebounded as though it had struck an invisible shield, and Josh himself fell.

"Josh, are you all right?" Sarah cried.

"Yes. But something's wrong. My sword didn't even—"

Dave brought down his own sword on the wizard's chair, and the same thing happened to him.

And then a voice suddenly filled the room. "And so I have you all. This indeed is the end of the Seven Sleepers."

"It's the Dark Lord!" Josh whispered. "I've heard that voice before!" But then he cried out, "You'll never defeat Goél!"

"You fool! Goél is doomed, and so are you!"

The chair began to vibrate, and Josh could feel the power of the Dark Lord draining energy from his body. At the same time he heard banging on the door behind him. He heard Reb say, "Something's happening to me. I'm losing all my strength."

"The arm of the Dark Lord is longer than you think, you fools!" The voice sounded triumphant. "Now you will die, and your precious Goél can sing his stupid song about the Seven Sleepers, but he will be lost also!"

Beorn felt drained of strength. Fairmina, at his side, was now on her knees, struggling to notch an arrow as if she could put it into the chair.

And then the voice of Goél sounded in Beorn's head. *The sword! The sword! Use the sword, Beorn!*

Beorn looked down at the blade in his hand. It was glowing with a white glow. With the last of his strength he staggered toward the crystal chair. Lifting the sword high over his head, he breathed a cry for help to Goél and brought it down.

A tremendous flash of blue lightning lit up the chamber. The air was filled with the crack of thunder and the cry of the Dark Lord.

And then the chair began to disintegrate!

"The chair! It's falling apart!" Josh cried. He had fallen to his knees, but now, oddly, he found his strength returning. "It was the sword! Goél's sword. You've done it, Beorn!"

The chair seemed to slowly dematerialize, and then it was gone.

"You really did it!" Reb called out. "I'm feeling strong again!"

One glad cry after another went around the chamber.

"The wizard is dead, and the power of the Dark Lord over this land is broken," Beorn said quietly.

At that moment Josh realized that the door was standing open. The spell that kept it sealed had been broken. One by one, warriors began to stumble in. They looked as if they were men who had waked from a dream, and they made no attempt to attack.

Beorn said, "Why, it is *you*, Kilnor!"

That warrior said, "My lord Beorn, I don't understand. I think I've been bewitched."

And thus it turned out that the slaves of the pale wizard came out of the spell he had put them under. Many of them were of the Yanti tribe, and Beorn welcomed them gladly. Others were of Fairmina's tribe. One was a childhood friend, who had been lost and she had thought dead.

"Have you been here all this time, Feanor?"

"I do not remember, Princess. I know it was like a bad dream. The wizard—" He stared at Zarkof's body.

"He kept us here by the power of the crystal chair. We were all enslaved."

"You're a slave no longer," she said. "The power of the pale wizard is broken."

"Then what shall we do now?" Feanor asked. He looked at Beorn—a man who had been his enemy. "We are all here, both Lowami and Yanti. Are we still at war?"

In the silence that fell over the chamber, Beorn took the hand of Princess Fairmina. "There will be no more war. Gather all together, and we will go first to my father and then to the father of the princess. We shall tell them that the power of the evil Dark Lord is broken."

A yell of victory went up, and soon all of the former servants and slaves of the pale wizard were gathered in the upper great hall.

"There are so many of them," Beorn said.

"Yes. Enough to follow our lead. May I speak to them?" Fairmina asked.

"Of course."

The speech that the princess made was one the Sleepers would never forget, nor would the warriors who listened. Nor would the man who later became her husband. She spoke of peace between the two tribes and of how war had destroyed them for long enough. Finally she said, "There will be no more war."

"But what will Chief Balog say?" one of the Yantis asked.

Beorn spoke up then. "When my father sees what has happened, I think he will listen to reason."

"Then, come. It is time to heal the land."

What took place next would fill a large book. The army of former slaves marched first to the Yanti village. There Chief Balog stood speechless as his tall son, standing with the daughter of Chief Denhelm, told what had happened. He looked around at the many men he had thought were dead and could not find words to speak.

And then his father, Magon, said, "Son, it is time for you to be wise."

Balog nodded. "Yes. Yes, I see that I was wrong to ever trust the wizard. We will not follow the Dark Lord any longer. We will stand for Goél."

The same scene was replayed when the warriors led by Chief Balog and his son appeared before the village of the Lowami.

Denhelm and his wife stood at the head of what men they had in their small force of defenders.

But Balog cried out, "We come in peace!"

Denhelm lowered his sword, and joy came to his eyes. Then he saw his daughter hand in hand with Beorn, the son of Balog, and he went to the Yanti chief. "My brother," he said, "this is good."

Balog looked at the two young people, then said, "I am ashamed of what has happened."

"We will put the past behind us," Denhelm said. "It looks as though our two tribes will be united even closer."

Balog smiled. "That means we will be related, does it not?"

"Yes. We will be brothers indeed."

A great cheer went up at this.

Abbey said, "Look! Beorn's kissing the princess!"

"Well, what did you expect him to do?" Jake asked.

Indeed, Beorn did kiss the princess, and there was great rejoicing in the land and among the Sleepers that day—the day when the Yanti and the Lowami became one tribe.

17

The Adventure's End

The Sleepers claimed that the wedding of Princess Fairmina to Beorn, son of Balog, was one of the happiest occasions they could remember.

It certainly was a time of rejoicing for the Yanti and the Lowami. Both tribes had suffered greatly from the war, and when the wedding guests saw their respective chiefs, Denhelm and Balog, embrace and pledge their loyalty to one another, a great shout of triumph sounded.

The Sleepers stayed long enough to properly celebrate the wedding, which, according to both tribes, took a week. And then Josh announced, "I had a dream about Goél last night. He told me that it was time to leave."

"Well, it's been great," Jake said, "but I'd sure like to get warm."

Reb nodded. "Me too. I'd like to go somewhere in the South Seas. Put on swim trunks and just lie in the sun and be waited on by both of you girls. That's the life for me."

"That'll be the day," Abbey sniffed, "when I wait on you, Reb Jackson!"

And so, as the warm weather came on, the Seven Sleepers said their last good-byes to all the friends that they had made in Whiteland.

A happy, radiant Fairmina embraced them all. "Dear friends," she said, "promise us that you will come back."

"It would be our joy, Princess." Josh surprised himself by taking her hand, then bowing and kissing it.

Beorn gave them all rich gifts and shook the hand of each one. He kissed the hands of Abbey and Sarah, and finally the good-byes were over.

The Sleepers made the return journey quickly, for the snow was now gone and they could travel on horses, the gift of the two chiefs.

The first night, as they made camp, Abbey seemed to have something on her mind. She was sitting with Dave after their supper. Suddenly she said, "Dave, do you think Fairmina is as pretty as I am?"

Dave was accustomed to Abbey's vanity. "Fairmina's as pretty as you, but not as pretty as I am."

"Oh, you're crazy!"

"I guess so. No, she's beautiful, and you'll be just as beautiful when you get grown up."

Sitting off to one side, Josh and Sarah giggled, for they had heard this conversation.

"That Abbey, she's a caution," Josh said.

"Well, I think she *will* be as pretty as Fairmina when she grows up."

"So will you, Sarah."

"What a nice thing to say."

"Oh, I'm getting a little more romantic. I remember what you said."

"*I* saw you kissing Fairmina's hand. I never saw you do anything like that before."

Josh blushed. "I don't know what made me do that."

"I do," Sarah said. "Josh, you've just got a natural sweetness in you that I've never seen in any other boy."

Without a word, he reached over and took Sarah's hand. He kissed it and then saw that *she* was blushing.

174

"That tears it. I'm getting as bad as Abbey. Just romantic as all get out."

"You have your moments, Josh Adams. You have your moments!"

For a long time, the two sat side by side, just looking into the fire. Josh found himself wondering, *What will be the next adventure for the Seven Sleepers?*

Moody Press, a ministry of the Moody Bible Institute,
is designed for education, evangelization, and edification.
If we may assist you in knowing more about Christ
and the Christian life, please write us without obligation:
Moody Press, c/o MLM, Chicago, Illinois 60610.

Get swept away in the many Gilbert Morris Adventures from Moody Press:

"Too Smart" Jones Series

Join Juliet "Too Smart" Jones and her homeschooled friends as they attempt to solve exciting mysteries. Active Series for ages 7-12.

Dixie Morris Animal Adventures

Follow the exciting adventures of this animal lover as she learns more of God and His character through her many adventures underneath the Big Top. Ten Book Series for ages 7-12.

The Seven Sleepers

Go with Josh and his friends as they are sent by Goél, their spiritual leader, on dangerous and challenging voyages to conquer the forces of darkness in the new world. Ages 10-14